FAST MAN ON A PIVOT

FAST MAN ON A PIVOT

by

DUANE DECKER

WILLIAM MORROW & COMPANY

NEW YORK · 1951

Seventh Printing, April 1969

FAST MAN ON A PIVOT

CHAPTER

1

In front of him was a palm-fringed archway from which floated a huge sign that said: *Welcome to Glensota, Florida, Training Camp of the World Champion Blue Sox—the Team of Stars.*

The last four words sharpened the sense of defeat which still clung to him after five years. They were true words; that was the trouble. If the Blue Sox hadn't been exactly that, a team of stars, he would have been playing in the big leagues these past five years instead of kicking around in the minors, condemned by the sportswriters' faint praise: a good journeyman ballplayer.

Bud Walker shrugged in unhappy remembrance as he drove his dilapidated roadster through the archway, feeling much as a presidential nominee might feel on approaching the White House grounds on a sight-seeing tour a week before election.

When the broad boulevard narrowed and bent abruptly left, he slowed down. There, in full view, was the picture he had carried in his mind for five long years—the rows of scattered stucco buildings, glaringly white in the burning sun. In the distance he saw the deep blue of the Atlantic and smelled its unfamiliar saltiness, mixed with the equally unfamiliar rich heaviness of the tropical flowers. And finally he spied, beyond the edge of town, a small piece of the sprawling mass of wooden buildings, once Navy barracks but now the spring headquarters of the Blue Sox.

The golden streets again, he thought. They still held the same magic they had held for him the other time the Blue Sox had called him up—the only call they had ever given him, as things had turned out. Until now.

I was cocky then, he thought. I wish I could feel cocky today. But now I know better. Now I know the difference between a good ballplayer and a star.

The golden streets led him through the small, sleepy heart of the town. At the main intersection he looked hard for the drugstore he remembered hanging around with other rookies, imbibing malted milks and engaging in contests of skill on the pinball games. No drugstore stood there now, however. In its place was a shiny supermarket, its spacious show windows gleaming with oranges and grapefruit.

That annoyed him vaguely for a moment and

he didn't know exactly why. But then it came to him. He resented any change in the town, because it served to remind him of the five lost years, of the money and fame and big-league excitement that had gone down the drain. Not because he hadn't been good. Just because he hadn't been super-good —a star.

But this year, finally, should be his year. The big, unsurmountable block that had faced him for the past five years was removed now. The gate was open. He was back with the Blue Sox to stay—or else he was through for good this time. Everything favored him now, yet even as he contemplated this pleasant fact, a small trickle of uneasy doubt nagged at the back of his mind. The gate had been open five years ago too, until fate, or whatever you wanted to call it, had suddenly lowered the boom.

A familiar hiss from his radiator caused him to swerve almost automatically into a handy gas station. He jumped out of the car and strode toward one of the water cans. He was a solidly constructed young man, neither noticeably short nor conspicuously tall. He wore tan gabardine slacks and a chocolate-colored sports shirt, open at the throat. His hair was cut crew style and his face was tanned to a light mahogany, because he had driven with the top down almost all the way across the country. His grayish-green eyes were clear and sharp, his face lean, and the strong hands, that could wrap around the handle of a 34-ounce Louisville Slugger with ease, were already calloused and hard from carefully disciplined winter sessions with an ax. He moved with the swift, catlike motions natural to all good second basemen.

He was emptying one of the water cans into the radiator spout when the gas-station man walked over. "Do anything for you, Mac?"

Bud stared at the man with a funny feeling that he knew him. The man had a sort of modified version of a handle-bar mustache and an extremely long, narrow face. But Bud couldn't place him.

"Nothing, Pop," he said. "Unless you want to buy a good secondhand car."

"*That* one?"

Bud nodded. "Don't laugh. Maybe it's shy on paint and stuff, but it's got a prewar steel top." He grinned, and added confidentially, "Cost me ninety even, and carried me across the country with no trouble except for this radiator. I'll sacrifice it for fifty, because I don't figure to need it any more."

Pop lifted the hood. He poked around inside for a couple of minutes. Then he glanced at each of the tires as he sauntered around the car. Finally he said, "I'll give you forty cash if you want to make it a spot sale."

"It's a deal, Pop—if you'll give me a lift from here to the Blue Sox training camp."

"You a ballplayer, huh?" Pop said, sudden doubt in his eyes.

"That's right."

"Son," said the man, "I'll give you a lift out there if you want to sell me the car. But I don't advise you to sell. I always tell them that when they show up here. You'd be surprised how many hopeful kids do that when they blow in from the West for spring training. But the Blue Sox are a team that's all clogged up with stars. Most rookies that come here still need a car when training's over, to head back to Moline or Council Bluffs or wherever they go to play ball for the summer."

Suddenly it came to Bud where he'd seen Pop's face before. Right here. Five years ago. He had done the same thing then—sold the jalopy. And when it was over, as Pop had said, he had headed West on a nonstop trip to oblivion.

"Don't worry about me," he said. "I've been here before. I know the score. So let's see the color of those forty bucks, Pop."

Pop shrugged. "O.K. then. You look older than most rookies, at that."

"I'm no rookie," Bud said. "I'm what they call an unarrived veteran."

"Then you know what you're up against. You know they turn out ballplayers in the Blue Sox farms like an assembly line turns out cars."

"I know. I just came off their conveyer belt myself."

"Well, come on inside the office and we'll make out a bill of sale."

They made out the bill of sale, and Bud pocketed four ten-dollar bills. Then Pop told the youngster who was fixing a flat to drive Bud out to the Blue Sox camp.

"Good luck, son," he said. "If you're in the market for another jalopy later on, look me up."

"Not me," Bud called back. "It's my year, this year, Pop."

Even as he said it, he realized he was not exactly coining a new phrase. He had used the same one five years ago. Hearing it now was like hearing a familiar record which had been played over and over again.

CHAPTER

2

———————

HE HAD PRACTICALLY MADE AN ANTHEM OUT OF that phrase five years ago. He remembered pretty clearly the first time it had popped into his mind. "That's my boy!" someone had called. "Bud Walker! Hey, Bud!"

It had happened downstairs in the training-camp cafeteria. It was his second morning there on that first trip up. He was living in a room with three other rookies who had also arrived from the long, tall brush, also bursting with the same sort of belief in their ability to beat the Blue Sox system of a star at every position. They slept in old Navy double-deckers, and Bud had drawn a top deck. It was rugged, that rookie life in the Blue Sox training camp.

In the morning you had to get to the lavatory early or else stand in line a good long while. You went down to breakfast in your baseball suit and slippers, carrying your spiked shoes under your arm. The chow line usually stretched all the way through the lobby. They threw everything at you, short of a dog tag.

When Bud heard his name called, he had just seated himself with a tray before him loaded down with juice and cereal, bacon and eggs, toast and milk. He looked up and saw the round, pleasantly pushed-in face of Bugs Boff, the Blue Sox scout who had spotted him playing in the Cherry Valley League two years before and affixed his name firmly to a Sox contract.

"Bugs!"

Bugs sat down beside him, beaming. He said, "Now fancy meeting *you* here."

"Yeah? Where else? Aren't you the guy I remember, a couple years ago, telling me this was where I'd land after a year in Double-A?"

"I said it," Bugs admitted. "And here you are. You can't miss, either, kid."

That was when Bud first used the phrase. "It's my year, this year," he told Bugs.

Bugs nodded his head hard, up and down. He reached over and purloined a strip of bacon that was especially crisp.

"You want to get stabbed with a fork?" Bud said.

"Buddy boy," Bugs said, munching the bacon contentedly, "you can get seconds, thirds, and even fourths. It's on the house. Plenty more where that came from."

"And plenty more hungry Joes in the line, too."

"Now what I tracked you down for," Bugs said, "is I wanted to tell you some good news. Ought to make you relax, it's that good."

"About McNulty?"

Bugs nodded quickly. "Guess you know McNulty looks more like a second baseman than anyone else the Sox have got. But old John never could hit his way out of a paper bag. He was just fast in the field. He's not even that now—showed up here fat and slow. Right now he looks more like a billiard player than a ballplayer.

"Give me a week," Bud told him. "I'll open some eyes around here."

"You have already. Jug Slavin asked me last night, he said, 'How about this green kid of yours, what's-his-name, who's supposed to be such a fast man on a pivot?' And I said, 'His name isn't what's-his-name, it's Walker.' Then I told him plenty."

Green kid in your hat, Bud thought. And that was the good thing about it, that year. He was young, twenty-two. He was young and as chesty as a fife-and-drum corps marching down Main Street on the Fourth of July. He had the world on a string—that year.

Bugs had kept talking, bubbling with optimism. It would be a big thing for him too, if Bud took over second for the Sox. His discovery. His boy.

But Bud had stopped listening. He was staring through the cafeteria into the lobby, where he saw

familiar faces—familiar from their newspaper pictures. There was Vic Valenti, the dark, quiet All-
Star center fielder, talking with Bix Hanson, the
big right-handed pitching ace. Plopped in a leather
lounge chair, reading the paper behind a screen
of cigar smoke, was Marty (Beef Trust) Blake, the
tent-sized first baseman whose big black bat was
a magic wand which, when waved, turned baseballs
into distant specks in the sky. Reading the paper
over Blake's shoulder was the veteran McNulty.
McNulty looked fat in the waist and worried in
the face—an old pro who knew his number was up.

Well, he wouldn't worry about McNulty. And
what else was there to worry about? It was this
year for Bud Walker, all right.

And as the training days settled into routine, his
confidence had grown. He was doing nothing
wrong in the field and he was hitting reasonably
well; he knew that many eyes were dazzled, among
the players, sportswriters, and fans, at the lightning
speed with which he made that vital double-play
pivot.

Even before the intra-squad games came to an
end and the exhibition schedule started, he had
supplanted McNulty on the Regulars and McNulty
had supplanted him on the Yannigans. Even Mc-
Nulty himself had conceded defeat. Bud found
that out one day from McNulty himself.

It was during batting practice and Jug Slavin suddenly called to McNulty to go to the mound and toss them in. "It'll limber you up," was what Jug called, but everyone knew it showed how far Mc-Nulty's stock had dropped. Pitching batting practice was menial stuff.

McNulty picked up his worn glove, walked listlessly out to the mound, and stooped to get some balls from the leather bag lying there full of them. Only the deadwood pitched batting practice: coaches, rookies going nowhere, and old-timers.

Bud was the batter. He watched McNulty put two balls into his glove. Then McNulty lobbed one in and Bud slashed it into left field. McNulty threw another one straight in and Bud belted it into center. On the third one, McNulty tossed it wide and Bud popped one up in front of the plate.

McNulty seemed to be deep in thought before he threw the next one in. It was wide again and Bud rolled it weakly down to second base. Again McNulty threw wide and Bud popped it up. After that McNulty tossed them inside and over, and Bud belted them freely.

It was perhaps fifteen minutes later when Mc-Nulty was relieved of his pitching chore. As soon as he walked off the mound, he headed toward Bud, who was standing alone near one end of the dugout.

"Kid," he said, almost gruffly, "I noticed something about you, pitching to you. You don't time those outside pitches the way you time the others."

Bud nodded. "I wasn't meeting them right. I knew it. But I didn't know why."

"I'll tell you why," McNulty said. And then he not only told Bud; he showed him, with a bat in his hand. He showed him how to wait on the outside pitch, to allow time to pick and choose, to hold back the inner eagerness like a good poker player.

When McNulty was all through, Bud said, "Thanks," but McNulty just shrugged and said, "It's something you'll need to know in this league or the word will get around."

That was all McNulty said, but Bud knew it was the fading veteran's way of conceding the job.

The Sox broke camp and headed North, and it became by then an accepted fact that Bud Walker was the new Sox second baseman. It remained that way, too, when they reached home, ready for the opener. It was, in fact, just two days before the opening game that Bud got the bad news—so suddenly, so unexpectedly, that there was no chance for anyone to tell him. It was there in the paper for him to read without warning at breakfast.

The headline on the sports page that stared up at him when he opened the paper was still sharp in his mind. It probably would be always. It said, "Sox Get Shore From Clippers in Four-Player Trade."

That was it. He didn't need to read further to know that the job he had earned the hard way had

been snatched from him—because this was a team
of stars, and Shore was a star. He was rated as the
best second baseman in the league. All-Star games
were incomplete without his name in the line-up.

No one needed to tell Bud that the wide-open
gate had suddenly been slammed shut in his face.
But someone told him soon enough. It was Jug
Slavin himself who gave him the word when he
reached the park that morning.

"Kid," Jug said, "I guess you know if the front
office hadn't suddenly swung this deal you'd be my
second baseman."

"I—I thought the job was mine."

"But now we got Shore. I don't need to tell you
about Shore."

"No," Bud said. "He's not just good. He's great."

"That's right. I told the front office I was satisfied to go along with you. But they weren't. They
want a big star at every position and . . . well . . .
you're a few years away from that."

"I know."

"It means you've got to go back where you came
from, kid. But there's this consolation: you're very
young and Shore is thirty. He'll fade in a few years.
And then. . . ."

"I'll be ready," Bud said. "I can wait a few years
if I have to."

"Good boy. And I'll be keeping track of you."

Perhaps he really did keep track of Bud, but the

years slipped by and Shore didn't fade. Not until last year. Then his speed was gone and his timing was off. The Sox called Bud up late in the season and he got into a few box scores. He saw that Shore was through. He knew that next spring, finally, he would get the chance that had been snatched from him before. He was not a kid any more, but he knew a lot.

It's my year, this year, he had kept telling himself all winter. And it had to be. If anything blocked him this year . . . well . . . it had better not. He had passed the kid days; he had no more years to waste. It was getting late, as a ballplayer's life span went.

CHAPTER

3

So now he was back here once more, standing at the main desk in headquarters building. He was a man this time, not a boy, and even if the muscles in his legs had grown a trifle knottier, his head was wiser.

The Sox classification system still listed him as a rookie, but with a difference: he was listed as a rookie in the highest bracket, one whose name was put on the Sox roster instead of on the farm-club roster. He could skip the business of filling out the detailed card that the raw boot had to fill out.

Instead, he sat down at a desk and filled out the camp registration card.

NAME: *Harold William Walker*
HOME ADDRESS: *8 Violet Lane, Bedford Springs, Nev.*
NOTIFY IN CASE OF INJURY: *Mrs. W. Walker, mother, same address*
DATE OF BIRTH: *February 19, 1924*

Position: *Second base*
Room Number: *64, Hq. Bldg.*

He didn't get a chance to see the other card filed under his name. That one listed the full scouting report on him. It had been filled out by the head of the Blue Sox scouting system, based on reports from Bugs Boff and three other Sox scouts. It read:

Height: *5-11*
Weight: *172*
Age: *27*
Arm: *Strong*
Fielding: *Above average*
Hitting: *Adequate*
Power: *Light*
Running Speed: *Good*
Aggressiveness: *Excellent*
Definite Prospect this year? *Yes. Inside track.*
Habits: *Good*

It was going on in training camps throughout Florida and Arizona and California, this cataloguing and cross-cataloguing of young and untested baseball talent. It was no more hit-or-miss than the sales campaign of a tooth paste manufacturer.

Bud followed two other rookies to the supply room, where he signed for two hand towels, one bath towel, two sheets, one pillowcase, and two blankets. He remembered how cold it could get sometimes in Florida, no matter what the chamber of commerce claimed. On top of that went his baseball equipment: pants, belt, shirt, stockings, and cap. He signed for these too. The other things— cleated shoes, undershirt, sweat shirt, and baseball socks—he had to provide for himself.

In time, he knew, he would have a roommate— one this time, instead of three—but none had been assigned as yet. At least he guessed not, for his room was empty when he got there. This room held two sturdy metal beds once used by Navy air officers. There were two small closets cut in the thin walls, and between them hung a faded print of a river with the sun peeping over a mountain behind it. It was labeled "Sunrise In Vermont." A washbasin filled one corner of the room; a small writing table filled the other. This was home for the training-camp period. It was not a very lavish home, but it was a big step up from the one he'd had the last time. A rule sheet lay on the writing table.

7 A.M.: *All personnel will be called.*

7.30: *Breakfast served in cafeteria (until 8.45).*

9.00: *Calisthenics on assembly grounds under direction of Coach Tweet Tillman.*

12.00: *Luncheon—served until 2 p.m.*

5.30: *Dinner—cafeteria doors close at 7 p.m.*

11 P.M.: *Lights out—all players must be in their rooms.*

The sheet contained other rules and other warnings. It told him to conserve food but to eat all he wanted. A neat trick if you can do both, he thought, considering the extent of his normal appetite. It warned him not to smoke in the cafeteria or the lecture halls. It made it clear that gambling or drinking would get him in more trouble than he could hope to handle. It pointed out that roughhousing, especially in the shower rooms, frequently led to injuries that damaged a player's future. It told him to take off his baseball shoes before entering buildings and never to leave the playing field without asking permission of Manager Jug Slavin. And finally, when the sheet had run out of advice and warnings, it said in big capital letters:

IT WILL PAY YOU TO HUSTLE HERE.

That was the picture, the pattern, that he remembered so well. He knew what training camp was: not the breeze, the soft touch that people seemed to think. It was a dull, relentless grind, a tougher day-in-and-day-out job than most. People who thought baseball players lived the soft life just didn't know much about it. Physically and mentally it was a murderous grind.

He went to bed early that night, and when he woke in the morning the room was so cold that he shivered on his way to the closet for his uniform.

He dressed fast and hurried downstairs to the cafeteria. He saw no one he knew, which was hardly surprising, so he ate alone at a table as close to the food counter as he could get. He remembered that angle—sit close enough to get seconds in a hurry.

Mail call was at eight-thirty. At nine he was in the Sox clubhouse, along with the rest of the army of both regulars and rookies, idling before his locker, killing time until Jug Slavin showed up to start the first of the daily meetings.

Finally Jug emerged from his small cubicle of an office. His familiar long-jawed face, with the thrust to the chin that had come, probably, from years of arguing with umpires, looked as restless as a combat lieutenant's, ready to brief a platoon. He was flanked by his three coaches. There was gray-domed Tammany Jones, who had been Jug's right-hand man from the start; there was Fido Murphy, who had been around almost as long; and Tweet Tillman, the Sox first-string catcher for years, until last season when age and infirmity had finally caught up with him.

"All right, boys," Jug said, "we start today and we mean business from the first pepper game. Do what you're told. Use your eyes and ears out there. After calisthenics come pepper games, then batting practice. Ask Tweet here when you take your turn for the hitting. He's got the batting order."

That was all. As Bud headed toward the door,

following the crowd, somebody standing just inside it grabbed his arm. He turned and found Bugs Boff beaming at him.

"You feel fit, kid?" Bugs said.

"Like a Stradivarius."

"My boy!" Bugs said cheerfully. "We make it this year, Bud. It's our year."

"It better be."

"It *is*. Shore's really through—not even reporting."

"Is that straight?"

"I got it right out of the feedbox, from Jug himself. No use trying again, he said. Asked for his unconditional release and got it. Nothing to stop you this time, huh, Buddy boy?"

"No," Bud said, "not a thing."

But, he was thinking as he trotted out onto the field, there hadn't been a thing to stop him at this time five years ago. The catch was, this was called the team of stars and they weren't fooling about that. He hadn't realized it five years ago. But he realized it now.

CHAPTER

4

YOU CAN TELL A HUNGRY BALLPLAYER BY HIS BATTING-practice look. He doesn't saunter casually to the plate and, with an amiable, unruffled air, give the crippled lobs a ride. He hurries into the box like a man in danger of missing a train, and he wades into the pitch as though a batting championship hung on every one. And if he ingloriously pops one sky-high above the infield's skin, he doesn't smile at himself in quiet amusement; his eyes narrow and his mouth tightens. He is not laughing off his badly timed swing. He is mad at himself and he doesn't care who sees it.

Then, when he's finished his turn, he doesn't stroll idly into the shade of the dugout and crack jokes. He doesn't dawdle at the water cooler, either. Instead, he strides impatiently to the bench, grabs his glove, and heads toward the field on the double, to shag balls for the hitters who follow.

Bud Walker had picked up these hungry habits because he was twenty-seven and still a minor-leaguer. The years in Triple-A exile had pounded into him the discouraging realization that he was just a good journeyman ballplayer fighting for a place among the stars. Hustling could help erase the difference a little. And hustling had become such a dogged habit with him that he didn't know how to play ball any other way, not even in practice.

But this year he had no star in front of him, and the qualities that were his to give this team were good ones. Maybe they weren't the qualities that would make him a star, but he could fit into this picture and do no harm to the team. That was what he thought as he leaned on the support pipes behind the backstop, soaking up the good Florida sun and impatiently waiting for his turn in the batter's box. He looked around him at the training camp that had been the place of his bright young dreams, and he wished he could shake off the awe that he felt for it and for the team that would be slowly welded into shape here.

It was, surely enough, a baseball plant vast enough to inspire awe. It was a plant fed by the huge, sprawling farm system that produced the Blue Sox pennants that kept the big wheel spinning.

Now, as the routine of the Grapefruit season was getting into motion, the place looked very much like a factory, with the automatic pitching and batting machines, the sliding pits, the dormitories, the blue sky specked with flying baseballs, and the clusters of scouts, coaches, and sportswriters hanging around. It was big business, this Sox organization, so big that it was no wonder even good young ballplayers could get swallowed up by it and never find their way into a starting big-league line-up. He, if anybody, ought to know.

A week had slipped by now. The exhibition games had not started, but batting eyes were getting sharper. He had picked up a roommate, Ed Mansfield, a tall left-handed first baseman built more like a tennis player than a ballplayer. But Mansfield had a fine Southern Association record behind him. He could hit and he was a fancy Dan around that bag. Mansfield was taking his practice swings now and Bud studied him, just as he studied all hitters in his spare time on the field.

Mansfield faced Eddie Lasky, the Sox' steadiest pitcher, who, amazingly enough, was a converted shortstop. Lasky was throwing fairly hard and his control was good even this early. Mansfield dug in, fouled the first one, and then caught the ball on the fat of his bat. He drove it to deep right center. Lasky came in with another juicy pitch and Mansfield promptly plastered it on a line to the same spot.

Behind him, Bud heard Tammany Jones speaking to Tweet Tillman as they passed.

"Looks like the Southern Association didn't change that kid. His power is still pretty much straightaway. He still doesn't seem to pull the ball."

"But it's fair power for a kid with no more meat on his bones than Mansfield."

"Yeah. He'll add power as he adds weight. But he'll never be another Beef Trust Blake."

"No. Never."

There it was again, Bud thought. Mansfield looked wonderful out there. Mansfield was every inch a big-leaguer. But he wouldn't be one—not this year and maybe never. He was simply banging his head against a brick wall known as Beef Trust Blake, one of the great stars of the game. Mansfield was doing everything right, even flawlessly, yet he would be heading back to the Southern Association in a few weeks.

Mansfield stepped out of the cage and Vic Valenti stepped in. Bud was due to follow Valenti, and as he waited Mansfield stopped beside him.

"You look cool," Bud said. "How do you do it?"

"This sun is just so much candlelight to me," Mansfield said. "You should play a double-header some Sunday afternoon in Mobile. You'd find out what heat is then."

"It's almost lunchtime," Bud said. "At least we don't have to wrestle through those calisthenics the way we did after breakfast. Playing ball under this afternoon sun is bad enough. Push-ups and stuff would be murder."

"It's good training for me—for Mobile."

"You're looking good," Bud said. "Hitting solid balls."

"Have you seen Blake hit them?"

"Well . . . yes."

"Anyway, I must be doing something wrong," Mansfield said. "Because they got me down for a session in the batting cages this afternoon. First time I've faced Overhand Joe and I don't look forward to it. Somehow, I'd rather hit against a man than a machine."

"Me too," Bud said. "I was in the cages yesterday, hitting them off the tee."

"How was that stuff?"

"You feel sort of silly, like you're playing golf. I guess I made out, though."

He could have put it more strongly than that. When he walked inside the cage, Tammany Jones had sized him up with a quick look, then adjusted the tee, a rubber contraption which looked something like a standing ash tray. Tammany had adjusted it so that it split the plate with the ball resting level with Bud's knees. After he had hit four balls off it that way, Tammany moved it forward and higher. Another half-dozen drives, and he moved it again. With each change of position, Tammany also made changes in the height of the tee.

Bud felt that he had done fairly well, even before Bugs Boff quoted the report Tammany made on him later at the meeting of the Sox brain trust.

" 'This Walker is really something to watch off the tee. Pretty level swing. No great shakes on power. But neat. He wasn't hitting right at first, but when we moved the tee forward he caught on fast and started to hit in front of the ball good. He doesn't have any real fault and catches onto everything quick. The boy can be worked with. He listens. He does what he's told. He's sound stuff.' "

His name had come up again, said Bugs, when Tweet Tillman reported the day's work on the running track and in the sliding pit. " 'Walker runs like a fullback, with a lot of drive, piston style. Not exceptionally fast but fast enough. He's what I call a hard runner. He isn't afraid to slide. He'll go in there any way you tell him to, and go hard. I think he'd be out there sliding yet if I hadn't chased him away, so I could work with some of them who needed it more. He's a good man. I like him. When do I get him again?' "

And finally, Bugs had given him Fido Murphy's angle. Fido had watched the actual batting practice, swing by swing, and had made notes. " 'Walker's a right-handed hitter whose power is limited and mainly to right center. Good stance, feet far apart. Takes a short stride. Good swing, level and quick, and he holds his bat steady. Might have most of his trouble with curve-ball pitching. He'll need some help there.' "

If it hadn't been for Bugs, Bud would not have

realized how every little move, every slight action
that he made all through the day, was being caught
and noted and classified by someone. No wonder
that only the very cream of the crop managed to
get through a training-camp grind. It was like working out in a goldfish bowl.

Valenti finished hitting and Bud stepped in. He
smashed Lasky's first pitch into right center. Not
deep, but in a game it would have found the hole.
Then he slapped one on the ground straight through
the middle that made Lasky jump in sudden panic.
He slapped one to center, one to right. He was
looking fairly stylish and he knew it.

When he ended his turn with a trickling bunt
down the third-base line, he heard Jug Slavin's voice
ring out from the bench. "O.K. out there, quarter
past twelve. Once around the park for everybody
and then in to chow."

Bud sprang toward the dugout and dropped the
bat. He grabbed his glove and lit out toward right
field and the first lap around the park. He could
feel the tempo of the training camp speeding up
day by day, and the muscles in his legs were loosen-
ing up along with it. Maybe he wasn't a ballplayer
who could make the big splash. But he was earn-
ing points in his favor the only way he knew—the
slow, hard way.

CHAPTER
5

THERE WAS NO OTHER WAY FOR BUD BUT THE SLOW,
hard way and he knew it by now. His early days in
professional ball had shown him that the headlines
were not for him. Neither was the wild acclaim
of the home fans. But pitchers always liked him and
for a very simple reason: his greatest talent, even
though it so often went unnoticed, was one that
made them look good. He was double-play insurance. He was a fast man on a pivot.

No big-league ball club shooting for a pennant
ever gets far with a second baseman who is a faint-
heart on the pivot. Teams that win somehow manage to put a whirling dervish of a man on the field
and turn him loose around second base.

Bud knew it was no coincidence that the second
basemen who showed up on the pennant winners were all fast men on a pivot. It gave him a
pretty fair notion of how important his talent was,
even though it was not the kind that made a splash.
He knew that in his quiet way he could do the

things that had to be done around that bag. Some
second basemen made the tough plays and made
them look just as tough as they were; he made the
tough ones and usually they looked easy. The pitchers told him that. Pitchers were his good friends
and appreciators.

He could go deep to his right behind the bag for
a treacherous smash and get it. He could charge in
for a slow dribbler without wasting a precious second to straighten up, and he could get it to first in
time, with a quick, off-balance snap of the wrist.
But even more important than making these second-
base plays, he could gobble up the wide, hurried
throw from third or short and then, while weaving
his body clear of the charging runner intent upon
taking him out of the play, he could get the ball to
first in time to complete the double play.

He was aware that he made the double play in
a fashion different from that of most of the second
basemen he had watched. Generally the ones he
had observed—even the good ones—did a sort of
dance step on the pivot, taking either a forward
stride or a backward skip off the bag. He called
that the "rumba pivot" and looked down on it. It
was far too slow to suit his style. He never made
any step at all—forward or backward. That lost the
precious second. He never even looked at the on-
charging runner, clearly bent upon his personal
destruction. That lost the precious second, too. He

knew that second base, more than anywhere else, was the spot where games were won by split-second ball handling or lost for the lack of it.

His style hoarded the precious second. If the runner was right on top of him, about to break up the play with a football block or a roaring slide aimed at his legs, he had a sure solution that called for superdexterity. He made a high jump straight into the air, then a quick snap throw while still suspended in this battle against gravity, and finally the drop down—giving the overaggressive runner a quick and warning worm's-eye view of his spikes.

It didn't take the Blue Sox pitchers long to spot this comforting touch of genius behind them. No one had to tell them what it could mean in terms of the tight ball games they would sweat through in the pressure-packed days of September.

"That Walker," said Bix Hanson, "gives me a nice sense of security."

"He's jet-propelled on the pivot," said Lasky.

"With him on second and the bases loaded," said Yank Yoland, an old Sox war horse, "I may even spring my curve ball on those lefty hitters."

But of course that only pleased the pitchers; it didn't stun the crowd, it didn't make colorful copy for the sportswriters, and it didn't make Bud a star. It just meant that he was giving something pretty important to the team and, since there was nobody around who could give anything more important, the pattern seemed set. This time he would be the Sox second baseman.

But he was keeping his fingers crossed. Two weeks had gone by now. The exhibition games were starting. The men were being separated from the boys.

"I'm sore all over," Bud said to Ed Mansfield after dinner. "I'm going up to the room and rub myself down, inch by inch, with liniment. And hit the sack early."

He had reason to be full of aches. It had been an especially tough day. Hitting off the tee, hitting against Overhand Joe; bunting, over and over again, until he could carom six out of a dozen balls into the four-foot circle drawn in powdered lime between third and home; sliding furiously in the pits, with Tweet Tillman goading him on; running on the straightaway track in match races under the gun of Coach Fido Murphy; and, finally, playing part of two scrub ball games. Even in the morning his legs had been sore, from yesterday's workouts. But the quick stops and starts all day long had punished his muscles until now they throbbed in rebellion.

He found, when he finished his session with the liniment and climbed into bed, that he was too tired to fall asleep. He was lying there fully awake when Ed Mansfield walked in.

"Bud?" Mansfield said softly.

"Uh-huh."

"You awake? Good. I've got news."

Suddenly the uneasy feeling came back to him. He felt the thing they called a premonition. Things had been going too well, too smoothly. You didn't break into the Sox line-up this easily unless you were a Blake, a Shore, a Valenti. He opened his eyes wide and looked at Mansfield. "What—what's the pitch?"

"You're on the squad going to Miami tomorrow to play the Clippers," Mansfield said.

Relief started to spread inside him. He had expected this. It didn't exactly stun him with surprise. Still, as long as it wasn't bad news. . . .

"They just posted the list on the bulletin board," Mansfield said. "You get the bus right after breakfast."

"Good dope." He sat up, and said, "How about you? You going?"

"Nix. I stay here to play with the B squad."

"That Blake. . . ."

"Sometimes I think it would be a better break to be owned by a second-division team."

"No. You just say that. You'd rather have a crack at playing with champs. Of course, I'm luckier. I've got no Blake in front of me now."

Mansfield was silent then and he looked away. The uneasy feeling crept over Bud again.

Finally Mansfield said, "I held out on some other news, Bud."

"A—a trade?"

"The Sox signed a bonus baby today. A twenty-one-year-old kid named Devlin. Six clubs were after him. The Sox gave him forty thousand bucks to quit college and sign. He's a second baseman, Bud."

Somehow he had known that a block was coming. Somehow he had known that, no matter how well he played, the Sox would still try to get a real star. It was their system. A real star at every position. Money was no object.

He knew all about this bonus kid, Joe Devlin. He had read about him off and on—an acrobat in the field, a powerhouse with a bat. The scouts had all claimed that if he would quit college, he could make the jump from the campus to the big leagues without any apprenticeship in the minors.

"Don't let it throw you, Bud," Mansfield said. "He's green, remember. He may not be as good as they say."

"Forty thousand bucks," Bud said. He thought of the seven years he had sweated out in the bush leagues for chicken feed. He thought of the chicken feed he would still be making this year, even if he stuck with the Sox. Five years ago it had been Shore. This year it would be Devlin. And against this fabulous bonus kid he would stack up as six years older, short on power, short on acrobatics. There was only one little trump that he could see clearly as his own: Devlin couldn't possibly be

as fast a man on a pivot. But it was a weak trump
that only the pitchers might possibly rate above the
three trumps that Devlin held. He shut his eyes
and tried to go to sleep, because his mind was beginning to fill with bitter thoughts.

CHAPTER

6

BUD RETURNED FROM MIAMI ON MONDAY WITH THE team, to find a note at the desk for him from Ed Mansfield. It said:

Dear Bud,

Well, mate, I got the ax over the week end and am on my way to another glorious season in the League of Lost Souls where the sweat flows so freely you think you're a trout, come August. Maybe the indestructible Blake will be a nice guy and break a leg. If so, I'll be seeing you. If not, I'll be reading about you. The Golden Boy can be cut down to size and you're just the pro who can do it. Use your influence to get me some World Series tickets in the fall. One of these years I'll get off the conveyer belt too. You'll see.

Cheerfully yours,
Ed.

He frowned and read the letter over a second time. Ed's attempts to be breezy didn't quite come off. He knew how Ed felt. Getting sent back, when you knew you were close to the peak of your form and style, was a damaging thing to the inner confidence. There was nothing to do about it when you were caught in this tangled net of stars except try to laugh it off. But that wasn't too easy.

As he turned to go to his room, he heard his name called. He looked around and saw Burt Kelly, the road secretary of the Sox, heading toward him. The red-faced Mr. Kelly wore his perpetually harried expression.

"Walker," he said, as he reached Bud, "your roommate has departed."

"I know," Bud said.

"So you've got a new one. I put this bonus kid in with you on account of him having too high a rating with the front office to be shoved down with the raw kids."

"Why did you have to put him in with *me*?"

"Everybody else had a roommate. Anyway, this is supposed to be one big happy family."

"Well, if that's what you're trying to prove, this is certainly the acid test."

As Bud headed upstairs, he couldn't rid himself of his feeling of resentment. He knew it wasn't Devlin's fault; it was the fault of a system. The kid, at twenty-one, had already made more money out of baseball, without even putting on a glove, than he had made after seven years in the minors.

And now Devlin would be the favored one for the job that Bud had sweated through those seven years to get, because Devlin represented a big lump of Blue Sox money, invested in a gamble.

He entered the room trying to wipe the resentment out of his mind, mentally preparing himself to like Devlin. But he found, quickly enough, that Devlin was not an easy kid to like.

The Golden Boy was sprawled out on the bed nearest the window. That was Bud's bed; he and Ed Mansfield had flipped a coin to see who got it. Now Devlin, coming in two weeks late, had simply taken it over. The room itself, which he and Ed had managed to keep in fair order so that neither one would create extra work or confusion for the other, was now a hopelessly confused litter of Devlin's personal belongings.

His two new pigskin traveling bags were open on the floor, so that you had to walk around them when you came in. Both chairs were heaped with fancy sports shirts and slacks. There were a half-dozen sports jackets carelessly tossed across the other bed. A set of golf clubs, a portable radio, and many pairs of shoes were a few of the things Bud noticed on the floor as he stepped around the pigskin bags. Devlin had the portable going full blast, with a silky-voiced crooner hard at work. He was reading a book called *Championship Golf.*

Bud gave him a quick study. He was big and

solidly built, thick through the chest and shoulders. His hair was very blond and wavy. He wore white buckskin shoes, light-blue slacks, and a pearl-gray sports shirt. He looked and acted unlike any ball-player that Bud had ever known. He also looked and acted like a very cocky kid who was used to doing exactly what he pleased, when he pleased, as he pleased. But, trying to be fair about it, Bud thought that getting a forty-thousand-dollar gift at the age of twenty-one might be apt to give any kid a sense of being a specially privileged person.

The newcomer looked over the top of his golf book. "Walker?" he said.

"That's right," Bud said. "Glad to know you, Devlin. Heard a lot about you."

"You'll be hearing more," Devlin said. "I'm in this business to mop up fast. If I can make my pile quick enough, I can get on to the game I really like." He tapped the golf book.

Bud stared at him. "You mean you really don't *like* to play ball?"

"The way I look at it," Devlin said, "it happens to be a game I'm good at. It's a fast-money deal. I like anything that's a fast-money deal."

Bud said, "You sure don't talk like a ballplayer."

"Well I'm enough of a ballplayer so I don't have to spend half my life batting around the bush leagues."

Bud just kept looking at him. Even if Devlin

weren't the man who was the big threat to his job, he could not have liked him. Devlin spoke the truth. He wasn't in baseball for love. He was in it for money. And as far as Bud was concerned, even if Devlin made the team and hit .400, he still wouldn't be a ballplayer. He'd be just a shabby imitation of one.

Bud said, "By the way, Devlin, that's my bed you've got there."

"Listen, old-timer," Devlin said, "don't try to throw your weight around with me. When I came in, this room was empty. First come, first pick. This is my bed."

Bud's resentment suddenly turned into a hard core of anger. "Devlin," he said, "if you're going to live with me, you'll get your stuff cleaned up around here, you'll haul yourself off of the bed that's been mine for two weeks, and you'll be careful of your personal remarks. Is that clear? Because I'm not in the habit of being pushed around."

Devlin got up and headed toward the door. "I don't take that kind of talk from a bush-leaguer. You're just sore because I showed up when you thought the second-base job was yours. Well, I'll be on second base for the Sox opening day, I'll guarantee you that."

"If it's a grudge fight you want," Bud said, "then you've got it."

Devlin slammed the door. He was back in fifteen

minutes with Burt Kelly and began to throw his
clothes into the suitcases. Kelly said, "I'm switch-
ing Devlin and a lad on the next floor. From what
he says, I guess you don't want to room with him."

"You guess right," Bud told him.

CHAPTER

7

THE VERY NEXT DAY AT THE PARK BUD GOT A FAIR taste of the situation he had to face. Devlin's antagonism was in his face when they met and it was in his voice when he spoke. A grudge fight for the job, with Devlin, would be a rough one. And the squad sensed the bad blood between the two very quickly.

Veteran ballplayers, on the whole, are apt to feel a certain resentment toward this new phenomenon of the baseball world, the bonus rookie, because baseball hands him, on a silver platter, the financial security they have all had to scramble years to get. But this resentment was not felt by the Blue Sox. This was a club used to winning pennants. They knew they had a gap at second base. They needed a star to replace a star. And if Devlin was the man, they wanted him to make good.

Bud's first look at Devlin in action convinced him that he was in for a dogfight. Devlin might be a kid with no professional experience, but someone had taught him a lot. And he had the natural grace, the poise, and the easy power of the born ballplayer. Bud studied him carefully in batting practice, before the start of a Varsity-Yannigan game. He wasn't the only one who watched the Golden Boy. Pepper games all over the field came to a stop or slowed down abruptly when he took his practice cuts. Everyone wanted a close look at the kid the Sox scouting system had said was worth forty thousand dollars.

Bud had to admit that when Devlin took a cut at the ball it was pretty to watch. Line drives left his bat as though exploded by gunpowder. Outfield smashes soared in long, majestic arcs. Even when he missed on a swing, his body spun all around with such flawless symmetry in the follow-through that he looked almost as promising whiffing air as he did when he connected for the long wallop. Out in the field he was little short of an acrobat. He raced deep into right field for short fly balls. He swooped incredibly far to his left and right for potential ground-ball singles. His arm looked strong enough for a third baseman's, but a ballplayer who could cover that much ground could have covered third base from a rocking chair.

Bud was baffled momentarily as to why a kid fresh from a college campus could hit and field with such polished authority. Then he remembered reading that Devlin's father, in his time, had been a big-leaguer. That explained it. Because Devlin had the look of a kid who had been groomed for this since he outgrew his rompers.

It also occurred to Bud suddenly that he was something of an old man compared with Devlin. When he had been up with the Sox before, he could have matched Devlin spring for spring and stride for stride. But not any more—not quite. Devlin was truly a flash. Then, too, there was obvious extra-base power in Devlin's bat, power that Bud knew he could not hope to match. From the look of the Golden Boy, he would be good for twenty to thirty home runs a season. And the record books showed that Bud had hit five in his very best year. It added up to a gloomy picture, and Devlin's antagonism would spur him on. That antagonism probably had something to do with the fact that the chief differences between them showed up sharply without delay in the practice game that afternoon.

Bud played second for the Varsity and Devlin played second for the Yannigans. In their first times at bat, the comparison that Bud had foreseen was dramatically presented.

Bud batted first. It was the top half of the second inning, because Jug Slavin had him batting seventh in the order. He came up with Kennie Willard on third base and one out—a spot where a hit wasn't needed to bring in the run. A long fly or a deep ground ball would turn the trick. He connected. He hit solidly, on a line to right center. But the ball wasn't placed to find the hole and it wasn't hit deeply enough to allow the runner to tag up and score after the catch. The center fielder took it on the dead run, coming in. Willard, on third, faked a start for the plate to draw the throw, then held back. And it was a good thing, too: the throw came in, hard and true, and Willard would have been out by many feet if he had made the try. Pete Gibbs, the big catcher, followed with a deep belt to dead center field, a blow that would have brought the run in easily after it was caught—except that Bud had just made the second out.

Then, in the bottom half of the inning, Devlin stepped up to the plate with runners on second and third and one out. He disdained two wide ones, then pasted the two-nothing pitch squarely on the seams. It went soaring, high and deep, into left center. Only after a furious run did Vic Valenti catch up with it. When he hauled it in he merely threw to third base; there was no hope of keeping the run from scoring.

That gave the Yannigans a 1-0 lead, and it clearly showed the difference between the potential runs-batted-in power of Joe Devlin and Bud Walker.

It was a bad ball game all the way through for

Bud. Not that he did anything wrong. It was just
that everything he did was topped by Devlin. Bud
singled in his second trip to the plate; Devlin
doubled. Bud raced toward the right-field foul line
after a pop fly deep behind first and dove for it, but
it eluded his glove by inches; Devlin raced for one
behind second base a few innings later and he dove
too, rolled over, and came up after the somersault
with the ball in the webbing of his glove.

It looked sensational and it was sensational. The
fact that it had really looked like the right fielder's
ball seemed to be noticed by no one except Bud
and the right fielder, who jumped hurriedly out
of the way when he saw Devlin giving it the acrobatic treatment. The look he gave Devlin was not
one of pleasure, but with the fans roaring their ap-
proval of Devlin, he didn't register any disapproval
beyond the look.

Later, in the dressing room, there was a buzz of
conversation about Devlin's play, and a good many
of the regulars stopped by his locker to speak to
him. They showed no resentment of the big bonus
that the club had paid him—not when they thought
in terms of another pennant and how this fast, long-
ball-hitting kid might help them win it. Bud
suddenly had the feeling of being a little like yesterday's newspaper, already half forgotten in the
rush of excitement over the newer and bigger news

of Devlin's arrival. He showered quickly and walked alone to the cafeteria.

On the way in Pete Gibbs caught up with him and said, "I'm early too. Eat with me."

They went inside and sat down. Bud felt pleased that the big first-string catcher had singled him out this way. But after they had finished eating and started to talk, he found out why.

"You've come up the way I did," Gibbs said. "The slow, hard way. I thought I'd never make it and I guess that's what you're beginning to think too."

"Well," Bud said, "they don't call it the team of stars for nothing."

"Just don't let it throw you," Gibbs said. "It threw me for quite a few years. I began to believe I was nothing but a Double-A catcher, the way the sportswriters were claiming."

"What happened?"

Pete grinned. "It came to me, finally, that I was sort of a star too."

"As simple as that?"

"No. As a matter of fact, I'd never have made the grade without Tweet Tillman's help. He believed in me. I think he was the only man on the team who did. But because of him I quit feeling like a second-rater among stars. I quit feeling awed by everybody else. That's what you've got to do too."

"You think I'm awed?"

"A little bit, yes. At least, I think you're a better second baseman than you think you are. I think you'll do this team a lot of good, because that's what the pitchers think. Give this bonus beauty everything you've got in this dogfight. Will you?"

"That's one thing you can count on," Bud said.

Gibbs talked on, asking about the leagues Bud had played in, where he lived, how the hunting and fishing were out there. The time passed quickly, and when they were through Bud had more of the feeling of being a part of the team than he had ever had before. He guessed that was why Gibbs had done this. Gibbs had gone through what he was going through and he had been helped this way; now he wanted to help somebody else the same way. It was a tonic to Bud and he wished, afterwards, that he had not read the late sports edition of the local paper when he went to his room. It dampened the good feeling that Gibbs' talk had given to him. The report on the game said:

> The Yannigans trimmed the Varsity this afternoon, but Jug Slavin doesn't have to feel any discouragement about that. Because the backbone of the Yannigans was the new forty-grand bonus beauty, Joe Devlin, who just stepped in and took charge of second base as though he owned it. He has the earmarks of a take-charge guy.
>
> This big, fast, powerful kid indicates in a hurry that he may be able to make the direct jump from

a college campus to a big-league line-up. Devlin
has all the stamp of a natural-born star and he's
got real polish, which isn't surprising since his father
is an ex-big-leaguer who has been busy polishing
him up since he was in knee pants.

In four trips to the plate he singled, doubled,
walked, and flied out. His fly-out was a poke so
deep in left center that it would conceivably have
been a home run in some big-league parks where
real-estate values cramp the outfield space a little
more than they do down here.

Until the Sox managed to steal Devlin away from
the other clubs who were after him, Bud Walker
seemed like a cinch for the job. Walker is a sound
second baseman. But when you've said "sound,"
you've said everything. In Devlin you see the mak-
ings of a spectacular star.

Bud put the paper down and thought about how
it would really be the end of everything if he went
back to the minors again. He wasn't a kid any
more. This had to be the year, because if it wasn't
he would be tagged a permanent minor-leaguer.
The years were working against him now. Devlin
had the big edge—youth, speed, power. But there
was at least one part of the game in which he felt
sure he could still beat Devlin. That double-play
pivot. That would be the only chink in Devlin's
glittering armor, but a chink was a chink. A lot
might be made of it by a guy who didn't quit easily.

CHAPTER

8

MARCH SLIPPED INTO APRIL AND THE SPEED-UP WAS as noticeable as the pace of a car when the gear is shifted. The rookies, who had bloomed so brightly in the first days, somehow started to wither on the vine. Now they were packing their bags and stealing quietly off in ones and twos and threes, to places like Joplin and Lancaster and Granite City.

The Grapefruit League was in full blast. The screw in the clamp of big-league pressure began to tighten, bit by bit, with every game. The pitching was getting smarter and the fielding was getting smoother. Already managers' necks turned varying shades of crimson when a ball game was blown in the eighth. Every small move was made for keeps.

Outwardly nothing had changed the starting Blue Sox line-up. Walker's name was always in it. But there was a dogfight going on and, thanks to the press, it was no secret. No one seemed to think that Walker had the job, not even Walker. He saw clearly how things stood. Because Devlin was so

young and so green, Jug Slavin could not stick his
neck out too quickly. That, Bud knew, was why
he started the games and why Devlin always finished them. But Devlin was being talked about
and written about more and more. His stock was
rising and Walker's, if not descending, was standing
as still as a millpond on a breezeless day.

And then, finally, the game came along which
showed as clearly as a picture on a screen just what
thought processes were going on in Jug Slavin's
mind. It was the day the Sox played an exhibition
with the Clippers.

Against the Clippers, even exhibition games were
important to Jug Slavin. The Clippers usually ran
one-two-three in the league standings, and beating
them in the spring was not a feat that Jug took
lightly. "Beating those Clippers," he said, "is a habit
any team has got to acquire to win a pennant in
this league. The earlier we get the habit the better
off we'll be."

This game was a pitcher's battle going into the
sixth. It was scoreless. The Sox had two measly
hits to show for their efforts; the Clippers had three.
Bud popped to third his first time up. He grounded
to short on his second trip. When he headed toward
the plate in the sixth, the Sox had their first threat
going. It looked like the spot to make sure of the
ball game. There were Sox runners on first and third

with one out. A long fly would get the tie-breaking run in. Before he reached the plate, Bud heard his name called from the bench. He turned to see Devlin striding out, swinging three bats.

It didn't crush him, because it didn't surprise him. Everything had been pointing to this moment for weeks—the moment when Devlin's power would remove Bud from his thinly fortified position. From here on in, he knew, it would no longer be a case of Devlin chasing him. Now he'd be chasing Devlin.

As he passed Devlin on his way to the bench, the rookie gave him a brief horselaugh in passing. Bud stepped into the dugout and sat down, chin propped in his hands. The Clipper pitcher was a respectable left-hander. He made Devlin go after the first two, fouling both off. That put Devlin in a big hole, but he didn't look worried.

The Clipper southpaw's arm flashed wide and the ball shot in, across the letters and slightly inside. Devlin had sensed that he would try to slip the third one past. He swung and met the ball solidly. He loved an inside pitch. The ball took off. It soared higher and higher, deeper and deeper. There was no doubt that the runner on third would score after the catch. But there was a lot of doubt about whether there would be a catch. The left fielder stood with his back against the fence. He leaped. He missed.

The ball plummeted over the fence. And Devlin, running loose and limber as a young colt turned out to pasture, followed the two Sox runners across the plate. Score: Sox 3, Clippers 0. As Devlin ducked inside the dugout, someone called, "Pretty good sacrifice, kid." Devlin held up his hand, making a circle of his thumb and index finger.

It was not only this way he had with the suddenly explosive long ball that swung the sportswriters to his side. They had already nicknamed him the Comet because of his incredible speed behind second base. The dispatches that they sent home for Blue Sox fans to devour were slightly delirious when they wrote about the Comet. Or so it seemed to Bud when he read them.

Exaggeration or not, there was no getting around the fact that Devlin had captured their fancy. And once you captured the sportswriters' fancy, you had captured the fans' fancy too. Devlin, Bud figured, must already be the fair-haired boy of the Sox fans, even before they had set eyes upon him.

The day after Devlin's pinch-hit homer, the thing that had been inevitable for weeks finally happened: Devlin started the game; Bud finished.

When the winding trek north started, this new rotation held. The promotion acted like a tonic on Devlin. Extra-base blows showered off his bat with increasing frequency. His acrobatic dives in short right field dazzled everyone, with the pos-

sible exception of Chip Fiske, who played that field
and twice narrowly missed a collision with the
Comet.

"Take it easy, kiddo," he said to Devlin on the
bench one day, when they had just missed banging
into each other. "There are eight other men, remember."

"That's the way I play second base," Devlin said.

"I called, 'I got it.' When I call, 'I got it,' that
means I got it."

"On those kind," Devlin said, "you can take the
day off and go fishing."

Most of the bench laughed. But Chip Fiske
didn't.

Now the squad was shaved down close to what
it would be until the twenty-five-man limit went
into effect on May 15. Pennant talk already hung
faintly in the air. The problem posed by Shore's
departure had been replaced by a pleasanter one:
there were two good men to fill the job and one
would have to go.

The night before the team reached home for the
season's opener, Jug Slavin did his first direct talking on the subject to Bud. He called him into his
compartment on the train and he didn't waste
many words.

"Walker," he said, "I've got to say what I said to
you five years ago. Maybe you remember?"

"In a hazy way," Bud said. "Would you like me to give you the direct quotes?"

"This time I thought for sure you were my second baseman. But that front office is star-happy. Five years ago they got me Shore. Now they got me Devlin. Shore, of course, was bonded stuff. Devlin isn't—yet. But he's my second baseman when we open tomorrow."

"Well, it does sound like the place where I came in."

"You'll be around until May 15. After that we can't carry two second basemen. You *might* try to make a utility man out of yourself. That way, if it panned out, we could keep you for bench insurance."

"Listen, Mr. Slavin, I spent seven years making a second baseman out of myself. I don't quit now. I don't turn into a career bench-warmer. I'll stick by my guns."

"You're the doctor, kid. Just so you know how things stand."

"Now I know."

"It's a tough fate that seems to dog you. But be ready. If Devlin comes apart...."

"Don't worry. I'll be ready."

He left, wondering why he hadn't taken up some simple line for his lifework instead of baseball. Brain surgery, for instance. That stuff was probably a lead-pipe cinch.

CHAPTER

9

BUD STOOD IN FRONT OF THE DUGOUT ON THE RIM of a bright-green grassy island in the middle of a sprawling ocean of steel and concrete. This vast park, like the team that played in it, filled him with awe. He stared around, almost in small-boy wonder, at the massiveness of such a stadium. He had seen it once before, a brief glimpse he had carried in his mind ever since. This place held sixty thousand people and an undetermined number of pigeons. It was still so early on this opening day that only the pigeons had arrived in full force.

He could remember well the manner of his leaving five years ago: the crowd hoarse in its delight at Shore's arrival, and his own hard-earned record of brilliance in the Grapefruit League a minor and forgotten thing. He had left this gilt-edged stadium behind him, not completely sunk, for he had youth to buoy him up, but with his banners slightly lowered. That brief memory of this ball park and his being a small part of it had been the warmest possession of his baseball life so far.

Now the stands, double-decked to the foul poles, were dressed for the opener as gaily as a girl going to a prom, with the pennants flying in neat rows. Fans streamed happily through the yawning concrete ramps for their first excited look, because last September was long ago. The good smell of roasted peanuts and boiled frankfurters was back. A big band, with brass gleaming in the sun, blared "Take Me Out to the Ball Game" from deep right field.

It was opening day. Nothing like it, the veterans said. Not even the World Series.

Bud had never seen any other big-league parks, but he thought that none could be more breathtaking than this one. The brown skin of the infield looked manicured and sleek. The far-flung carpet of the outfield was a deep, rich green. The American flag on the center-field flagpole blew briskly toward the left-field corner and the brand-new, super-de luxe scoreboard in right center had slots to tell everything but the temperature.

A fan sitting in a front box behind the Sox dugout turned the page of his newspaper. Bud glanced at it in passing, on his way to the water cooler. He spied the big headline on the sports page: "Sox Open Against Grays With Devlin on Second." So there it was in letters as high as your hat. Devlin was big news. Devlin was a Golden Boy and no mistake. Thinking of the speed with which all this had come to Devlin and the futile years that he himself had spent battling oblivion, Bud felt an ache inside him like the turning of a screw.

When the bell rang, ending the Grays' practice and turning the field over to the Sox, he watched with an envy he couldn't hope to conceal as Devlin trotted out, flanked by Madigan, Bates, and Blake. The Comet looked as though he belonged, and perhaps he did. The crowd thought so: they roared a welcome at him.

Seven years was a long time to fight for a chance that never came; it was hard to stand idly by and watch someone else move in on it. So hard, in fact, that at the moment Bud could have chewed the lacing right off his glove. Instead, he dropped into the dugout and stared out at the practice session. He couldn't help but marvel at the flawless efficiency of this baseball machine whose letters he wore—for the moment, at least—across his chest.

Tweet Tillman, bat in hand, was banging grass-cutters at the infield, first to Madigan, then to Bates. And then he drove a hard hopper at Devlin. Devlin charged the ball, almost prancing, like a high-strung race horse. He played it on the hop that suited him, swooped it in, and shot it to Beef Trust Blake's waiting glove. Blake reached forward and flicked it in, the ball looking like a marshmallow in his big mitt.

Blake swung his oxlike body around and rock-eted the ball down to Pete Gibbs. The rangy catcher with the cowboy look slammed it down the middle where, at second, Devlin awaited its clothes-line flight. Devlin plucked it from the air, whirled, and snapped it down to Madigan, who crisscrossed it to Blake again. Back it went to Gibbs, who rolled it slickly off his arm into Tweet Tillman's waiting hand. With the bat, Tillman punched it toward Bates, and the dizzy pattern of the ball's flight was resumed.

Now Bud watched the outfield. Kennie Willard, the big Negro star in left, chased a long one back to the bleacher railing, where he released the hid-den springs in his legs and came down with the ball in the pocket of his glove.

In center Vic Valenti, the old pro, came in toward the second-base bag like a startled deer and reached down on the dead run to snatch one off his shoe tops. Then, out in right, Chip Fiske took one go-ing away, over his shoulder. At the crack of the bat he had turned his back and headed for a spot of which he seemed completely certain. Once there, he took his first look at the ball and discovered, to no one's amazement, that it was coming down right where he had figured it would. He pulled it in as easily as if he had used a long-handled shrimp net.

No doubt about it, Bud thought, this is a solid ball club—if it's solid at second.

Whether it was or not, the fans made it clear before the game even started that they thought so. Devlin had established himself as a big-leaguer with them by the sheer weight of his press clippings. When his name came over the amplifiers during the announcement of the opening-day line-up, it drew a bigger outburst than any other. It seemed to Bud that all the way down the line Devlin did not have to earn a thing. Everything seemed to be dropped in his lap.

Lasky, on the mound, was an extremely crafty operator. He didn't have blinding speed, but he had a cool head on his shoulders and seldom got behind the batters, making them go after the pitch of his selection, not theirs.

He looked in good form today. The first Gray hitter popped high to Bates at Short. The second one arched a fly close to the left-field foul line. Willard had a long run, but he was there with a last-second lunge that gave him finger-tip control of it. The third Gray hitter topped a slow roller between first and the mound—and Devlin made his first mark in a big-league box score.

He charged in. Traveling at top speed, he grabbed the ball. The batter, with only ninety feet to negotiate, had most of it in the wake of his flying spikes when Devlin reached the trickler. There was only one way to cut the runner down and Devlin used it. Still on the run, still at top speed, he flipped the ball across to Blake with an underhand snap. The throw had to be fast and straight. It was both. It beat the runner by an eyelash.

The crowd really roared this time. He was their boy; they backed only winners, and he had all the earmarks. Walking to the dugout, Devlin grinned at their sustained yells and tipped his cap. Anything he did would have been greeted with a roar. But this had really been a slick piece of business. The crowd, all sixty thousand of them, let loose.

Devlin, batting seventh, didn't get a chance to hit in the first. Madigan lined out to short left, Fiske looked at a third strike, and Valenti almost knocked the third baseman down with a ground ball that he played off his chest and strong-armed to first in time.

Lasky mowed the Grays down again in order, and the Sox came in. Blake, the clean-up monster, settled in the batter's box like a four-motored plane that has just taxied to the airfield's apron. He philosophically observed three balls go by and then, as usual not looking for a walk, he tied into the three-nothing pitch with a zeal that must have terrified the Grays' pitcher. The ball shot deep to the far reaches of center field. All center fielders played Blake as deep as if he used a carbine instead of a bat, and the Grays' man was no exception. But a gull could not have caught up with this one.

It hit the base of the center-field bleacher wall at the 430-foot mark and ricocheted crazily toward left, with two outfielders in mad pursuit. A modestly fast man wearing hip boots could have had an inside-the-park home run standing up. But Blake, whose waistline resembled a whale's, just managed to lumber into third with a triple.

Now the crowd woke up with the bang of a small boy on Christmas morning. Willard stepped in and, at two and two, lashed a wicked grounder to short. It was hit hard and deep, deep enough for a man on third to come in without breaking any speed records. Blake not only broke none; he found the ball clamped onto his leg when he slid. The slide had been manfully performed, but all it accomplished was to get his brand-new creamy-white uniform ready for the laundry call. He got up glowering accusingly at the umpire, who glared back as Blake rolled toward the dugout, trailer-truck fashion. Meanwhile, the speedy Willard had pumped into second.

Patsy Bates, the lean, agile shortstop, stepped in, eager to allay the crowd's frustration over the run that had slipped through their fingers. That first run of the season would have a special tang, unmatched by any of the hundreds to follow. But the best that Bates could produce was a sliced grounder toward right, which the Grays' second baseman gobbled up with neat dispatcn. Willard moved to third on the throw. Two outs now, Devlin stepping in.

If it had been officially Devlin Day at the stadium, with friends and relatives from his home town filling every seat, the ovation couldn't have surpassed the one he got. They screamed and whistled and stamped their feet. They had never seen him hit, but they knew he could not fail. He looked as good up there as the press clippings had advertised him to be. He stood with his feet spread wide, the bat loose on his shoulders, a cocky half-smile on his face. The muscles below his cut-off sleeves looked hard and formidable.

He went all out after the first pitch, but it fooled him. It broke sharply down and he missed it. His body spun around like a top and though he only connected with air, the crowd roared its delight, sure from the picture-book look of him that if he had connected, the ball would have found a distant resting place. It struck Bud that Devlin looked more picturesque whiffing air than most ballplayers looked hitting a grand slam.

Bud thought, He's a greater man in their eyes now than he was before. And what he did was just to get fooled like any green busher. Color, that's what it was, or what they called it. When you've got it, you've struck gold. When you haven't got it. . . .

The pitch came in. This one was high and Devlin let it go. The third one was low and, though Devlin started after it, he checked his swing in time and didn't break his wrists. Two balls and one strike now. Willard danced off third.

This time the pitcher came in with it—fast, letter-high, and slightly inside. Later on, of course, when the teams had swung around the circuit and the pitchers had got to know what the new hitters feasted on and starved on, it would be only a mentally retarded pitcher who threw one fast and inside to Devlin. But this was the opening game. This was an understandable mistake on the part of the Grays' pitcher.

Devlin saw it and swung joyfully. He had a toe-hold. His swing came from the heels. He met the ball squarely. The resultant blast was a thing of ferocious beauty. Some home runs are pop flies, aided by short fences and strong winds; others are line drives, mashied close to the foul poles, tidy but not terrific. This one, though, was pasted. It was high and it was deep. The wind was behind it, too. The ball was still skyrocketing when the Grays' left fielder gave up, his back pressed against the bleacher wall. It landed in about the tenth row, where a number of delirious Sox fans cheerfully pummeled each other black and blue trying to get possession.

Sox 2—Grays 0.

Willard was waiting at the plate to shake Devlin's hand. The crowd was on its feet, trying hard to lose both voice and mind. Devlin had made his press notices look feeble. His first big-league at-bat had tallied first hit, first home run, first two Sox runs driven in for the season.

Devlin dropped into the dugout. Somebody slapped him on the back and somebody else called, "That's the ticket, Devlin. Show Blake how it's done."

Devlin grinned, and said, "Blake? Who's Blake?"

Blake grunted.

And Bud thought, Golden Boy is right. Everything he touches turns to gold. But what's the name for my type, that makes everything turn to lead?

CHAPTER

10

THAT HIGH AND MIGHTY SWIPE OF DEVLIN'S INTO THE left-field seats was the spark that lit the fuse. The Grays were the orphans of the league, anyway. They hadn't scaled the dizzy heights of the first division for a good many years. Once their pitching staff was punctured, it usually collapsed like a tire with a nail in it.

Devlin, it developed, had punctured it deeply.

Pete Gibbs, next man up, picked off the second pitch and rammed it through the hole between left and center. When the smoke cleared, Gibbs stood on second with his arms folded.

Lasky stepped in. Lasky, having been a short-stop, was a hitting pitcher. He slapped one ju-diciously through the middle and Gibbs romped home. It was 3-0 now.

Madigan blooped a mean little thing into left that could not have been rescued by Houdini, and now men were on second and first and this two-out

rally began to look like a drama of serious proportions.

It definitely was one when Chip Fiske, cagey
master of the hit-and-run art, punched a deft
ground ball between first and second. As it squirted
through to the outfield, both runners, who had been
off and galloping with the pitch, advanced two full
bases. Lasky scored and Madigan breezed into
third. The score was 4-0 now.

Valenti rammed one with zeal into the extreme
left-field corner, good for two bases and two more
runs, as Madigan and Fiske raced across the plate.
Now it was 6-0, and the crowd was far too ecstatic
to sit down. In the minds of the fans this year's
pennant was clinched—in the second inning of the
first game of the season.

That was enough for the Grays' pitcher, a tardy
conclusion finally reached by the Grays' manager.
From the bull pen strode another bit of pitching
fodder for the Blue Sox cannons, an apple-cheeked
southpaw whose blinding fast ball was widely re-
nowned, but only among the readers of last year's
Twin Falls (W. Va.) *Gazette*.

Sixty thousand people were more than he had
pitched before in a whole season up to now, and to
find them all crammed in one park on one day was
startling. He faced the mighty Blake and showed
at once that he had a brave heart. He poured his
fast one in, determined not to flinch before the testi-

mony of the record books, a weapon which Blake always carried up to the plate with him in addition to his bat.

The Beef Trust was in no mood to take such insolence. He wafted his potent wand at this bold pitch and, though swinging slightly late out of sheer surprise, he rifled it to right center. It was belted, but it had two things against it: the fleetness of the Grays' center fielder and the wind, which still blew briskly toward left. It was finally speared on the dead run near the 400-foot mark. So the deluge was over.

When Devlin trotted out to his fielding position, the applause rolled over the park in waves. After it had died down, stray shouts followed from the stands.

"You sparked it, kid!"

"Nice eye, Devlin! Nice eye!"

"How to go in there, Champ!"

Bud sank deeper into the dugout seat, cushioned with foam rubber. Devlin couldn't have jumped off to a better start. Bud felt now like the famous fifth wheel on a wagon. Even if Jug Slavin by some miracle gave him a chance, this crowd would shout for Jug's scalp for keeping their boy on the bench. Devlin so clearly fitted into what they expected of their team: a flashy star in every spot.

Bud had thought this couldn't happen to him twice. But it was happening. It wasn't really Dev-

lin; it was the vast chain system that had licked him
from the start. But he wasn't quitting. Two innings
didn't make a season and one home run didn't
crown a man king. He suspected well enough where
Devlin's weakness was. And Devlin's weakness was
his own special strength. If no one else found it
out, the pitchers would. You could bank on that.

Bud saw it reveal itself in the fifth inning. It was
a small thing maybe, all other assets of Devlin's
considered, and yet it had in it the seed of team
demoralization. Devlin only made the easy double
play; he did not make the tough one. He was a
slow man on the pivot. In this game, of course, the
one he missed in the fifth inning made little difference. This game was wrapped up, tied in a
bundle. But in the dozens and dozens of games to
follow, the missed double play could lose many ball
games and break the spirit of several pitchers.

In that fifth inning the Grays, with one out, had
somehow managed to load the bases by means of
a single, a walk, and a beaten-out bunt. They were
behind 8 to 0 now and the situation was well in
hand, so what followed seemed of small importance.
The Gray batter banged a ground ball down to
Patsy Bates at short. It was deep but it was hit
hard. The way Bates covered his territory, it had no
chance of getting through. Bates swooped it in
and shot it to Devlin, at the bag, for the force.

Bud had spotted many second basemen, pros

though they were, who did not really know their job. He added Devlin to the list now. Here, under pressure, he was guilty of the same slowness he had shown in practice. There are two things a topflight second baseman does not forget for a moment. First, he must fire that ball really hard to first. The number of pros who fail to do this is amazing. It isn't always that they forget; it is just that some of them do not have the knack of doing it from off balance.

Devlin did not throw the ball hard enough.

Then there was the second vital thing so often missed, and Devlin missed it. He did not stay cleanly out of the runner's path. It is not an easy trick when a man tries to do it the orthodox way, as Devlin tried to do it. Because, with the throw coming to him—as it almost always does—from the third-base side of the infield, his back is to first base and to the runner. That means he has to pivot off his right foot, which Devlin did, and make the electrically quick throw to first as he strides with his left foot inside the base line in order to take himself out of the base runner's path. As usual, the runner came in determined to break up the play. He came, naturally enough, fast, hard, and with a slide that made a target out of Devlin.

There was only one way for Devlin to make the play work, doing it his way. He had to quick-pivot and make the throw at the same time that he crossed the bag—not *after* he crossed it. Bud watched tensely to see if Devlin did the little things he had to do. He had to charge so that his right foot hit the forward point of the bag as he pivoted off it toward first, and he had to step away from the bag *as* he threw. That stepping-away was vital, for it would carry him out of the runner's path. But Devlin did it wrong.

Devlin crossed the bag and tried to step away and *then* throw. Before he threw, the runner hit him. His throw was blocked. The double play did not come off.

The precious split second he had lost meant that the Grays were not retired, which would have pulled Lasky out of his hole and preserved his shutout. Only the runner at second was erased. The batter was safe. That left two men on, at first and third, and the first Gray run had slipped in.

Lasky was a trifle flustered and showed it on the first pitch. It was too good, and it was promptly laced down the right-field foul line for a two-run triple. The score was 8 to 3 now, with activity starting in the Sox bull pen. Then Lasky pulled himself together and struck out the next hitter to put the damper on the rally.

But after that he wasn't quite the same sure pitcher. When men got on the bases, he didn't look loose. And the fine edge of his superb control simply wasn't there. The Grays kept pecking away at him, inning after inning, and in the eighth they finally got him out with three straight singles. But the Sox kept hitting, too, and young Herb Ward came in from the bull pen to hold the Grays through the ninth. The final score was 12 to 9, a win for Lasky and for the Sox, but a badly pitched ball game. Lasky wasn't in the habit of starting strong and finishing weak. It was an off day for him.

Devlin wound up with three hits in five trips to the plate and no official error charged against him. The crowd gave him a farewell salute as he trotted off the field. Afterwards, down in the dressing room, the team seemed to have accepted him as completely as the fans. One by one, they stopped to tell him something pleasant about the game he had played. There was, in fact, only one man in the starting line-up who failed, as Bud noted, to chip in his word of praise. That man was Lasky.

CHAPTER

11

THAT OPENING GAME SEEMED TO HAVE SET A NEW pattern, not at all typical of the Blue Sox in the past. The pitching developed a nervous, high-strung tendency that kept baseballs constantly flying back and forth in the right-field bull pen. The heavy Sox hitting, however, counteracted the sloppy mound work. Not with finesse but with sheer brute force, the Sox swept the three-game stand against the Grays.

Bud rode the bench and watched. Mainly he watched Devlin. No small move the rookie made escaped him. By the end of the series he knew a lot about Devlin. But his own routine had fallen into a hopeless dead-end groove. He went to the field early every day and played around at second base through all the batting drills. He needed to do it to keep himself loose and at ease with his job in case a break came along. A month wasn't much time, but it was something, and if he couldn't do anything else in the way of putting up a fight, at

least he could keep himself at the ready. Beyond
that, as far as a fight for the job was concerned, he
might just as well have been a man in chains.

If Jug Slavin knew he was still around, he didn't
show it. Of course, Jug was on a spot where he had
to bend over backwards to give Devlin every preference. The front office had invested a sizable
amount of money in Devlin and they didn't want
the gamble to turn out wrong. Then, too, Devlin
had caught the home crowd's fancy so completely
that he was a real drawing card at the gate. People
were shelling out money for a look at the new star.

Certainly the home crowd, who had in any case
never seen Bud Walker play, had no desire to see
him now. To them he was a meaningless name in
small print at the top of the score card, an unre-
markable infielder who had batted around the bush
leagues for years. In all the time he spent shagging
balls in practice, no one ever called his name from
the stands. He was, in their eyes, as nondescript
as the bat boy.

That was the setup after three days. Even if
the Sox had lost those games, Bud doubted that he
would have been given a chance. But with the
sweep . . . well . . . managers seldom broke up winning combinations under any circumstances. Still,
he did not see how the Sox could keep on fashion-
ing victories in such a sloppy manner.

After that wild and woolly opener, they took the

second game from the Grays the same way, with loose pitching and heavy hitting. Only a four-run rally in the eighth pulled that one from the fire, 10 to 9. It was Bix Hanson, this time, who failed to last. The Grays teed off on him for a five-run inning, and in the middle of it Bud saw what he was sure should have been another double play slip through Devlin's fingers—one which would have choked off the rally. But no one else seemed to see it that way. The crowd was thrilled by the late surge, the long-ball hitting, and once again by Devlin. He splashed a gaudy double and a single. The team had won two straight. They were off and running. The crowd filed out in a very happy mood.

Then the Sox took the third game, thanks to four Gray errors and six walks by the Gray pitchers. The final score this time was 8 to 6. Yank Yoland, the Sox starter, lasted through nine innings, but he was jittery all through, and the bull-pen staff pitched nine full innings out there in right field.

A sweep was a sweep, though. The sportswriters who probed deeply enough to find something dubious about the sweep had an easy and comforting answer for it: the team hadn't quite settled down yet. No, they admitted, the Sox couldn't win a pennant this way. But their pitching was really sound. It would assert itself soon, as it calmed down. At this stage of the game, they said, the hitters were probably ahead of the pitchers. And Devlin, the Comet, was truly brilliant.

Brilliant, maybe, Bud was thinking, but not sound. Devlin made the outwardly flashy plays of the great second baseman, but he failed to perform the basic function. He was not a steadying influence on pitchers or infield. He was a loose part in the structure and even if the team didn't see it yet, they were feeling it. Bud would have bet on that.

He watched Devlin so closely that he couldn't have missed less if he had used binoculars. Devlin's inability to save that precious split second in the pivot which, Bud was sure, robbed the pitching of confidence and poise, was not his only failing. He was interfering with Chip Fiske, in right field, even as he thrilled the crowd with his acrobatics. He was overeager to show how much ground he could cover on the short pop fly. Fiske could not yell him off of a ball once he started for it. In the final game against the Grays, Devlin went deep for one. He made it, with a last-gasp lunge and somersault, and when he came up with the ball in his glove, it was pretty to see. The crowd roared. But Fiske did not. Fiske grew testy.

Fiske could have made the catch easily and he tried in vain to yell the Comet off. But when he saw that Devlin was keeping after it, he took a sidelong tumble to avoid collision. At the end of the inning Bud heard him speak sharply to Devlin at the water cooler, after Devlin had finished tipping his cap to the thunderous ovation the crowd gave him when he trotted in.

"Maybe you didn't hear me yell you off the ball?" Fiske said.

"I knew I had it," Devlin said with a grin. "I never miss those kind."

"Neither do I," Fiske said.

"What difference who gets it?" Devlin said. "An out is an out."

"All I used to have to watch was the ball," Fiske told him. "Now I watch the ball with one eye and you with the other."

"You'll get used to me," Devlin said. "On those kind you can just sit back and get fat."

But the team left home for the first brief Eastern swing in first place and with Devlin already being talked of as the rookie of the year. He was solidly established—and in three games.

Something had to happen, Bud knew, or he would be back in Triple-A without so much as a look. But he sat tight and waited. When you had already waited seven years, you didn't throw in your glove. You sat quietly, like a cat under a bush studying the movements of an unheeding bird, ready to spring hard if the right moment ever came.

The right moment didn't come on that first swing through the East. The Sox set off, eager to open a swift gap between themselves and the rest of the league—especially the Clippers, rebuilt with youth this year, and a team to fear.

The trip started out well. They took two out of three from the Chiefs, a patchwork of fading veterans. Then they moved into the Grays' home park and took two out of three there. They had quickly consolidated a lofty first-place perch now, with their seven-and-two record. But it was the slugging that had carried them all the way. When they moved into the Clippers' stadium and ran up against some first-division pitching, they fell apart.

It was a three-game series and the Clippers won all three games. This had never been the Blue Sox style: murdering the pushovers only to fold before the real competition. Their little lead was shot out from under them even more quickly than it had been constructed.

The pitching had settled down somewhat; it couldn't remain as shoddy as it had been. But it was far from being as good as it needed to be. The Clipper series made that as clear as chalk writing on a back fence, for two of those encounters had slipped into the games-lost column by one-run margins. The sting in a one-run defeat is far greater than it is in a lop-sided slaughter, because it is in the tight ball games that champions assert themselves. The ability to slam the gate shut in the face of the enemy's late-inning attack is vital for a pennant. The Clippers did it. The Sox didn't. There was an uncertainty about them in the tight payoff spots that was revealed in overeagerness and mild jitters.

"Two things," Jug Slavin told them after the second loss, "that we have to do to win a pennant. One, we've got to take those one-run ball games. And two, we've got to beat those Clippers. So far we're flopping at both, and don't tell me it's too early in the year to get excited about it. It's never too early when you're shooting for the big target. From the minute the first ball is thrown out on opening day, it's later than anybody thinks. It took me about twenty years to learn that the hard way, but I finally know it for a fact."

If he or anyone else suspected that second base was the root of the team's uncertainty, it was never indicated. And even Bud himself had to admit that if Devlin *was* the root of it, he had himself well screened. In the twelve games played so far, he was hitting a very stylish .331 and his extra-base power was gaining league respect. Slavin paid him the highly significant compliment of pushing him from seventh in the batting order up to sixth. He dropped Patsy Bates, who had a heavy cold he couldn't seem to shake, into the eighth slot and moved Pete Gibbs up to seventh. It was the first time within the memory of the earliest stadium settler that the Sox had owned a catcher with enough power to bat above the usual eighth place in the order. But big, rangy Gibbs had already shown beyond a doubt, in his first year as a regular, that he had arrived.

When the Sox returned home for the first long stand against the invading Western clubs, you could hardly say that outright panic had gripped them, but on the basis of the opening Clipper series there existed reasonable doubts that they would get far without a marked improvement. Three times, in pain and sorrow, they had looked at the Clippers and seen in them what they themselves had hoped to be: the team that swung the league's whip.

Jug Slavin summed it up for them in the home dressing room as the Sox prepared to face the Redskins, the first of the invaders. "The Clippers," he said, "showed what they had in the way they played us. They had daring and a reckless confidence and the ability to bounce back when they got behind. But, most important of all, they showed the ability to beat us. We've got to pull ourselves together and be a team, not nine men batting their brains out. And we've got to do it fast."

The opening game with the Redskins was hardly the answer. Patsy Bates was worse and did not even put on a uniform. Slavin used Frank Adams, a veteran utility man, at short. Adams had been a fine shortstop, and back in the days when McNulty had covered second for the Sox, the Adams-McNulty combination had led the league in double plays. But though Adams was still a cool and dependable performer, he could only wave at ground balls as they went by, balls that Bates would have put in his hip pocket. That was sadly apparent in the first Redskin game, which they won mainly by means of ground balls slapped through the middle and into the hole between short and third.

Bud watched, feeling a strange anger that was directed at nothing and no one in particular. He knew what caused it: the sense of being a man sitting in chains, helplessly watching a good team fall apart before his eyes. He had not been fully aware until recently how much the Sox meant to him. He had been one of these men now since mid-February. And here he sat, day after day, suffering through every enemy hit with them and unable to lift a finger. He thought, If I could just get in there —just once. I've been fighting for the chance so many years and never had it yet. Just once—that's all I ask.

It must have been a premonition. He was dressing slowly in the locker room after the fourth defeat, when someone touched him on the shoulder. It was Buster Stookey, the Sox bat boy.

"The sahib wants to see you," Buster said.

"Slavin?"

"Yeah. As soon as you get dressed."

Bud finished dressing in a hurry and went to

Slavin's small office, with hope rising in him. His feet on the desk, Slavin sat there alone, scowling at the walls.

"You ever play shortstop?" Slavin asked abruptly.

"My first pro year, a little," Bud said. "But. . . ."

"I know. You don't want to be a utility man. You told me that once. But this is different. I've got a hunch you could cover short better for the next couple of games than Adams can. I never realized how much he's slowed down, because Bates has never missed a day before. You want to try it?"

"Anything," Bud said, "is better than the bench."

"Can you get along with Devlin? I heard you couldn't."

"I can get along with Devlin. The question is, can Devlin get along with me?"

"Well, we'll see. You come out early tomorrow. Put in some time at short. A couple of the boys will come early—one to hit you grounders, another to play first. Get yourself feeling a little at home."

"How early?"

"Say noon. It'll only be for a couple of days. Bates will be back then."

Bud left in a hurry. Tomorrow afternoon seemed a long way off. He wouldn't be where he belonged, but at least he'd be in there. Jug Slavin probably didn't realize it, but this would be the first time, after seven years of shooting for it, that he had ever succeeded in breaking into a big-league line-up.

CHAPTER

12

"YOU WITH THE REDSKINS?"

"No, the Sox. I'm Walker. Bud Walker."

The little gray-headed man who tended the gate at the players' entrance looked Bud over carefully, then scratched his head in mild bewilderment. "My mistake, son. I should know 'em all. Been guarding this gate longer than I care to remember, but your face . . . well, somehow, I just didn't place it."

"Think nothing of it," Bud said. "Practically nobody but the paymaster knows I'm around."

Maybe, though, after today he would lose a little of this faceless anonymity that had been his ever since he had signed a Blue Sox contract. At least they'd find out he was a real person and not just a name printed by mistake on the score card.

It was early, not even noon yet, but Bud wanted to get out there early. He wasn't going to play his own position, but he was going to play. He wasn't going to be in for more than a day or two, but at least he was going to be in.

He strode down the big concrete tunnel, past all the hot-dog stands that weren't open yet, until he reached the doorway of the Sox dressing room. He walked inside and saw no one except Pickles, the clubhouse man, sweeping the floor. Pickles claimed he never understood where his nickname came from, which indicated that he was not a vain man, for he could never have remained baffled by it if he had studied himself in a mirror. He was dressed in khaki and wore a Sox cap. When Bud walked in, he merely grunted by way of saying hello and went right on with his methodical sweeping, the sucked-in expression never leaving his face.

Bud walked down the line of lockers until he came to his own at the end, and then he saw the big figure sitting on the stool near the cooler that held the soda pop. It was Herb Ward, the kid relief pitcher who could calm the jagged nerves of a capacity crowd merely by taking the long walk in from the bull pen. Herb failed sometimes to put out the enemy fire, but not often. Relief pitchers were usually veterans, and it was amazing to find one so good at the ripe old age of twenty-two.

"The big thing about Herb's pitching," Pete Gibbs had told Bud once, "is that he actually knows what he's doing. That's rare among relief pitchers. He can get that ball across the plate. He's got a fast ball and he lets a batter see it, but that's about all. They never get a chance to hit it, or practically never. He's got a lot of pitches, and when they're swinging he gives them his slider or his palm ball or his curve. But not his fast ball. Don't know how he learned so much at his age."

Herb called, "Hey, Walk! When do we start?"

"We?" Bud said. "You in on this session?"

Herb nodded and grinned his amiable, cocky grin. "When I heard what was up I asked to be your first baseman. Always wanted to play first. Anyway, I need exercise. Get fat sitting out in that bull pen."

Herb walked over to the cooler, picked out a bottle of root beer, and signed his indebtedness for it on the sheet tacked above. Then he selected a sandwich encased in wax paper from the pile placed there earlier by Pickles. He did not sign for the sandwich. The Sox had a system which no one had ever explained: the player paid for the soda, but the food was on the club.

Bud stripped and started to climb into his uniform. Herb munched away at his sandwich between swallows of root beer.

Finally he said, "So you're gonna play short today."

"The man says so," Bud told him.

"Ever play it?"

"Not much."

"Only like second, huh?"

"It's the only place I'm good at," Bud said, "but anything to get off that bench."

"At least you got a good seat. Out in the bull pen there's no foam rubber and you don't even see much."

The door opened again and Tweet Tillman came in, followed by Willie (the Lion) Simms, the bull-pen catcher.

"Want to play a game of rummy out there this afternoon, mate?" Herb said to the Lion. "I got my cards in my locker."

"Man," the Lion said, "the way things been going, you'll pitch nine full innings out there whether you get in the game or not."

Tweet said, "Snap to, men. Let us not be derelict in our duty. We have to turn a second baseman into a shortstop in less time than it takes to cook a hot dog." He heaved a long sigh. "Maybe we're on the track of another pennant, but so far I don't recognize any of the footprints."

Bud's orders were to take it easy, not to knock himself out. The idea was to get familiar with the new distances he had to travel for a ground ball, both to his right and his left, and also to the different way he would have to time his throws now that he was farther from first base. He waited, motionless, in the deep shortstop spot as Tweet and the Lion lumbered slowly to the plate, embroiled in a violent argument about the merits of a new ten-cent cigar.

"I like 'em because they're mild," the Lion was saying.

"Don't give me that, Lion," Tweet said. "You like 'em because they're ten cents."

"I got to admit," the Lion admitted, "that the price don't make me unhappy."

Herb Ward waited at first base impatiently, kicking the bag. "Come on, come on!" he yelled. "Plenty of time to argue when you get to the Old Soldiers' Home, and that's just around the corner for both of you."

Bud felt impatient too. He was eager, but not as tense as when he had arrived at the stadium for this session. Then he had kept thinking about the fact that this would be his first big-league start and in a strange position, too. But now he wanted to get going. This practice would be different from the regular ones. This one had meaning. It led to action, not to the bench. He punched his fist in his glove and glanced around behind him. A freckle-faced kid who would hawk peanuts in the stands later on stood there. He had been enlisted for this period to shag balls that went through to the outfield.

"How about it?" Bud called.

Tweet placed a half-dozen old balls in a semi-circle back of the plate. He held one in his hand. He called, "All right. Let's go, Bud. Show me, boy."

Then he sent one skimming straight at Bud, hit with care to take a nice even hop. Bud swooped it in and pegged hard to first. It was a low peg but Herb pulled it in, though not with the greatest of ease. As Herb heaved it on down to the Lion, Bud thought, Got to remember it's a longer throw from here.

Tweet cracked another one. It went to Bud's left. He grabbed it, and this time his throw was on the dime. Herb squeezed it.

"That's how!" Tweet yelled enthusiastically. "You catch on fast, kiddo."

Tweet kept banging them at him with merciless speed, wasting no seconds once the ball had traveled from him to Herb to the Lion. Bud darted left, then right, then in toward the mound. Sometimes, just before he laid his glove on it, Tweet would scream, "Home, boy, home! Big run a-comin' in from third!"

And then Bud would ram it on a line to the Lion's waiting mitt and the Lion would make burlesque motions of clamping it onto the hopelessly defeated runner coming in from third. They could have been four kids on a sand lot waiting for the call to supper, with all the easy chatter and the fantastic diamond dramas that were dreamed up with almost every fungoed hit.

Finally Tweet called, "Enough! Class dismissed," and Bud came trotting in from his position. He crossed paths with Herb at the entrance to the tunnel, just behind Tweet and the Lion.

Herb said, "Just what I needed to build up a little appetite. Let's have a sandwich, men."

"Sandwich!" the Lion roared at him. "Man, you just stuffed your stomach before you came out. What makes you eat so hoglike anyway? You sure don't do nothing, just sit out in the shade of that bull pen all day long."

"Don't forget I'm just a growing boy, Lion," Herb said, grinning, "and you're an old, old man." He turned to Bud. "That Lion, he's so old he's got three grandchildren playing outfield in the Three-Eye League. How about that?"

The Lion snorted. "The Lion," he said, with dignity, "is just climaxin' his twenties."

"You old goat," Herb said, "I'll bet you roomed with Abner Doubleday once."

The Lion made clucking noises. Tweet roared. And Bud felt good and calm and relaxed inside—not nervous and tight as he had felt earlier, thinking about his first big-league test. It occurred to him then that maybe there had been a reason behind all this aimless chatter and constant good-natured ribbing. These three men knew what it was like to play in that first big game. They knew it was better to do as little worrying and as much joking beforehand as possible.

It made him feel that, bush leaguer or not, he was among friends who understood. That in itself was a discovery, and a happy one.

CHAPTER

13

THERE HAD NOT BEEN MUCH GOOD-NATURED CHATTER lately around the locker room or in the dugout. The Sox already had the slightly haggard look of a pressure-ridden ball club. Usually that was a look which did not appear until September, yet now, on the first of May, the look was definitely there.

Bud had seen it ever since those nightmarish three days in the Clipper stadium. It was evident in the tight, set way they went about their practice drills and the manner in which they talked to each other, in monosyllables most of the time, with few laughs and little kidding. That sense of pressure showed in Jug Slavin's seamy face, too, for the problem of probing for the cause of the trouble was his. Two weeks did not make a season, but the storm signals were up. Blowing a whole series to the team they had to beat was a brand-new experience for the Sox.

What made it especially hard to understand was that on paper they looked stronger than last year, when they had gone on to win a pennant the hard way with a sudden-death play-off game after the regular season had ended in a deadlock between themselves and the Panthers. Now they were certainly stronger, with a rugged young catcher in place of old Tweet Tillman, who had limped in and out of the line-up all last season with a recurrent Charley horse. And last year Shore had slowed down to a walk in his hitting and fielding, while now they had Devlin, young and strong, hitting hard and traveling far and wide around the bag.

It didn't add up. It simply didn't make sense. No one knew that better than Jug Slavin. If this early collapse were not soon checked, the Sox would find themselves unable to catch up with the hustling Clippers, who had gotten off to such a fast start. And, besides the Clippers, there were the Panthers, who promised to be every bit as tenacious as they had been last year.

Bud crouched on the steps of the dugout and watched the final warm-up tosses of Harry Diefendorf, the Sox starting pitcher. Harry, known as the Hawk, was a tall, angular man who, off the diamond, always looked as though he would be more at home behind a plow than on the mound. His awkward, shambling gait gave no indication that once he toed the rubber he would become a figure of utmost grace and symmetry, with blinding speed in his long right arm.

The amplifiers made preliminary grating noises before the starting line-ups boomed across the field. Bud listened carefully. The sound of his own name would come out of them, boldly casual, for the first time. He strained to hear it. This familiar ritual might mean nothing to a Blake or a Madigan or a Fiske. But to him, this first time at least, it would be one of the biggest thrills of his life.

The names of the visiting team came first, and then the Sox. Bud leaned forward, not even trying to conceal his intentness as he listened.

". . . and for the Sox, Madigan, third base; Fiske, right field; Valenti, center field; Blake, first base; Willard, left field; Devlin, second base; Gibbs, catching; Walker, shortstop; and Diefendorf, pitching."

Diefendorf's name was almost drowned out in the quickly rising murmur of surprise that greeted Bud's name. Even though the fans had seen him follow Adams at short during infield practice, they had not expected it. Bud could imagine the rustle of score cards as they hunted through the list of names to check his and try to remember where they had heard it before.

I couldn't have attracted less attention for seven years, he thought, *if I'd put the time in as a waiter in a restaurant.*

The pitchers quit the warm-up, and the ground-keepers finished chalking the batter's box and dragging the infield back into a state of pool-table smoothness. And then, finally, Bud's big moment came. The Sox sprang from the dugout and trotted toward position. He found Devlin jogging along beside him and as they started to separate, near the mound, Devlin suddenly spoke to him.

"Say, Walker...."

"Yeah?"

"Don't play it as deep as you did in practice. You haven't got Bates' arm, you know."

Bud stopped dead and looked at him. "You play second, Devlin. I'll play short."

Devlin let out a whistle. "Let a busher into the line-up and all of a sudden he knows it all."

He was glaring at Bud and Bud glared back. They stood that way for a long moment.

Bud thought, Don't let him get your cork. That's what he said it for. To get you sore and throw you off your game right at the start.

He felt a hand on his shoulder and when he turned around Madigan was staring at him, looking both puzzled and angry.

"What's going on here anyway?" Madigan demanded.

"Nothing," Bud said. "Just an intellectual discussion. We both belong to the Book-of-the-Month Club."

"Well if you guys want to put on the gloves," Madigan said, "and go a few rounds, just speak up.

We can call off the ball game for you and play a double-header tomorrow."

Bud saw Jug Slavin up on the step of the dugout now, and he turned and trotted to his position in a hurry. His face felt warm and not from the weather. But he walked to the spot where he had stood in practice, the spot where Bates stood for a straightaway hitter with no men on.

A nice, brotherly double-play team we make, he thought. Mixing us together is like mixing a bottle of milk in a crock of pickles. But if Jug Slavin doesn't like where I'm playing the position, then Jug will say so. Or Madigan will speak up. He's team captain. But where does this Devlin get off? A green kid like that, still wet behind the ears, telling me where to play.

Devlin had wanted to rile him. Devlin wanted him to look bad. He would have bet his last sweat shirt on that.

Bud stood there waiting for the warm-up tosses, trying not to stare around at the stands. But it was hard to avoid, this first time. They weren't filled, but they still held the biggest crowd he had ever looked at from the field. They were half full at least, which meant thirty thousand people. He could feel a harsh, probing intensity reaching out from them. It gave him the momentary feeling of being a fugitive in the night, traced by a giant searchlight.

In an effort to shake it off, he gazed at Diefendorf, warming up. The Hawk threw eight warm-up pitches and then made an awkward ducking motion as Gibbs tossed the ball down to second, where Devlin took it at his knees. It shot around the infield then and finally went back to Diefendorf. The Sox pitcher held it in his glove as he bent and rubbed the resin bag between his fingers. The first Redskin batter stepped in.

Bud crouched, his eyes fixed on the plate. He saw Gibbs signal for the curve, and the Hawk nodded and toed the rubber. He took a quick glance around at his outfield and his infield, his eyes lingering on Bud a little longer than on the others. The Hawk always performed this rite as though he half expected to find part of his support gone, perhaps into the stands to buy peanuts or out to the bull pen for a quick nap. Reassured that he had a quorum, he faced his hitter and started the windup.

As the first pitch left Diefendorf's hand, Bud felt all the tenseness and worry leave his mind and body. He knew suddenly that the dread of anticipation was left behind and he was really in the game, lost in it as a diver is lost in the coolness of the water after the plunge, leaving the heat of the sun behind him.

He was no longer thinking of the size of the crowd, or the unfamiliarity of his position, or the mistakes that he might make. He had even forgotten the irritation he had felt toward Devlin. That was all gone. It was a funny thing and hard to explain, but he always felt far less tension playing in a ball game than watching one. Somebody had told him that it was the normal reaction of the pro and right now, in his first taste of a big-league game, he was glad to find out that he was a pro all the way.

The first pitch broke sharp and low. Bud saw the Redskin lead-off man go all the way around and he heard the ball crack into the pocket of Gibbs' big mitt. With that explosive sound, his glove automatically went to his mouth in a cupping motion and he shouted, "How to do it, Hawk boy, how to do it!"

All around him came the familiar rising buzz of the infield, each one chipping in with little strings of words that sounded meaningless in themselves but which, somehow, made a pitcher feel less alone than he really was, more a part of the whole force bearing down hard upon the batter. For standing on the mound with everything depending upon his own arm and head was what made a pitcher's job such a frightening and lonely one.

The Redskin lead-off man stood with his bat poised again, grimly intent upon redeeming his mistake. The Hawk uncoiled and came in low again, but too low, and the pitch went by for a ball. The Hawk threw high next time. Two and one. Then he came in fast across the letters and the hitter leaned against it. The ball took off on a screaming low line toward right field. The quick groan of the crowd suddenly lifted to a yell of joy as Devlin, sprinting furiously, leaped high and came down with the ball glued inside the pocket of his glove.

It hadn't been hard to get, actually. But it happened so fast, and the ball sounded so good when it left the bat, and Devlin had leaped with such a snap, like a jackknife springing open, that he emerged from the play looking sensational.

The crowd thought so. They told him.

"That's the Comet!"

"Nice eye, kid!"

"How to go!"

Then the Hawk let one slip and it hit the batter in the arm. He shook it off and trotted down to first, looking more pleased than pained.

The third Redskin watched the crafty Hawk just miss the corner on two in a row. Then he slashed at the two-nothing pitch and it shot into right field cleanly, on a line, for a long single. Fiske took it on the hop and only faked a throw toward third, where he had seen from the corner of his eye that the runner from first was heading. Then he snapped his throw to the waiting Devlin at second, to keep the batter from taking second as he had seemed all ready to do in case the throw went to third.

Redskins stood on first and third now with but a single out. The Hawk looked deeply troubled, as well he might. He took one of his doubtful glances at the men who stood behind him and then he stared at the Redskin clean-up hitter with the apparently malevolent hatred that always filled his eyes at the sight of any batter who faced him in a tight spot. Pitchers who didn't hate easily, Jug Slavin always said, luxuriated in many early showers.

The Redskin clean-up man glared back with equal ferocity, and the Hawk, taking no windup, caught the corner with a low curve to put himself ahead in the duel. The Hawk missed on his change-up, but then came in again, still firing low, and the hitter swung, but only fouled it off.

One and two now.

The Sox infield, drawn in somewhat on the first pitch in order to be set for both a play at the plate and a double kill, moved back to normal position. The Hawk reared back and slung his fast one, hoping to blow it by. But the Redskin batter caught it with great solidity and sent it spinning toward the hole between third and short. Bud had started with the ball. Madigan couldn't reach it. Maybe he could. With a burst of speed, he did. He scooped it up, backhand. It had been hit with such riflelike speed that, even though it was deep, a double play was written on it. Bud's instinct told

him that even as he heard Devlin yell behind him,
"Home! Home!"

No. That safe stuff was for fainthearts. Bud's
recklessness was mixed with confidence, a very
sound combination. He spun and shot the ball to
second where Devlin, waiting, grabbed it as the
runner charged.

Devlin crossed the bag in time, and the batter
was still steaming up the line to first. Devlin could
get him—could have gotten him, that is, if he had
released the ball as he crossed the bag. But as usual
he didn't. He crossed the bag and then he released
it.

It was still a photo finish at first, but the batter
won. The runner from third scored. Devlin wheeled
toward Bud as the crowd groaned. "Home!" he
snapped, "I told you, Walker! The play was home!"

"The play was where I made it," Bud barked.
"It was a D.P. ball. You held it until after you
crossed the bag."

Devlin advanced toward him, hands on hips, in
such a way that the whole park could see he was
bawling out the substitute shortstop who was just
somebody named John Doe to them.

"Don't pin your bonehead stuff on *me!*" he
shouted. His voice carried.

From the stands angry roars and prolonged boos
poured out, enveloping the field like escaping gas
fumes. Bud knew who was getting booed. It was

not their little gold-plated hero. The two of them stood there close together, glaring, when both Madigan and Blake reached them.

"Knock it off, meatheads!" Blake growled.

"Play ball and shut up," Madigan said. "You're in the big leagues."

Bud went back to his position and then Devlin did too. Diefendorf, in pure anger at the world in general, blew three straight strikes across the plate and the inning was over.

Jug Slavin was waiting for both of them at the dugout steps and his face was stony. "I've had enough," he said. His voice was so calm it lacked any inflection at all. "This team was in bad enough shape. Now we get childish brawls on the field. Last spring I put you two in the same room and that lasted about ten minutes. Now I put you on the same field and that's lasted no longer. Well, this public brawling didn't happen with Bates or Adams at short. So you take a shower, Walker. Adams will finish."

The triumphant look on Devlin's face made Bud long to hang one on him then and there. But that would finish him for good. Devlin was in the driver's seat and he might as well face it. He turned toward the tunnel entrance, rage and fury churning inside him. As he passed the bat boy he said, "Get my glove out there for me afterwards, Buster."

Then he headed toward the tunnel door and the

showers. The boos from the crowd swelled and beat down upon his ears so hard that he could almost feel a physical impact from them. But he didn't lower his head. He raised it. He hadn't done anything wrong and that was that.

Well, he thought, as he headed down the ramp, you finally broke into a big-league ball game, kiddo. And played a fine game, too. For a whole half inning.

CHAPTER

14

CHARLIE K. O'NEILL, THE PRESIDENT OF THE ENTIRE
Blue Sox system, had never divulged what the *K*
stood for, and as a result the more critical among
the sportswriters hinted that it stood for Kremlin.
For it was O'Neill, well screened from public ap-
proach by a battery of telephones, secretaries, and
thick oak doors, who made the decisions that shook
the Sox system to its farthest reaches and could be
challenged by no one. Jug Slavin's word might be
final law upon the playing field, but outside of it
he was just a puppet pulled about by the many
strings which O'Neill held in his hands.

It had been O'Neill who made the final decision
on the investment of the stockholders' forty thousand dollars in Joe Devlin. If Devlin should flop,
the crash of President O'Neill would be heard much
farther than the crash of the kid himself. But Devlin's fine start had thoroughly reassured O'Neill in
a long-held belief of his: that the shrewdest oper-

ator in big-league baseball was none other than himself.

Naturally, then, Bud knew the minute he got the word to report to O'Neill's downtown office that his little rhubarb with Devlin was being turned into a fairly celebrated affair. He guessed that his very presence on the roster, since the big investment in Devlin, had made O'Neill a little nervous. He could well imagine that it would ease O'Neill's mind greatly to have him out of the way and the field permanently clear for the Comet. With so much time and money sunk in the vast Sox farm system, O'Neill had suffered some harsh criticism for flinging bonus money around instead of coming up with a home-grown new second baseman. No one had to tell Bud that O'Neill was fighting for Devlin in preference to himself the way a mother eagle fights for her young.

Bud stepped out of the elevator on the second floor of the downtown office and walked to the end of the hall, where he entered the outer office of President O'Neill. There he confided his name to the regal receptionist who confronted him. He saw eyebrows lift down the line of lesser office personnel when he gave it.

The receptionist replied, as though conferring knighthood upon him, "You may go in, Mr. Walker. Mr. O'Neill and Mr. Slavin are expecting you."

She pushed a warning buzzer as Bud approached the paneled oak door behind which his personal destiny, for five years, had been treated like a ball of putty. So Slavin was in on the kill too. Bud did not knock. He merely took a deep breath, turned the knob and entered. When you went down for the final count, he thought, you might just as well go down swinging.

President O'Neill sat behind a glistening desk the size of a modest Hollywood swimming pool. Jug Slavin sat in a chair opposite the desk. O'Neill was a man of huge physical proportions and the tweed suits that he always wore made him look even bigger. He squinted at Bud through a blue film of cigarette smoke.

"Sit down, Walker."

The wave of his hand imperiously directed Bud to a chair in the corner. O'Neill kept staring at him through the smoke film. He had a feeling that this must be what it was like to get tossed into a police line-up prior to the grilling.

Finally O'Neill spoke. "I called you here, Walker," he said, "to tell you that the Sox are sending you down now, instead of waiting until the fifteenth. I made the decision, and Jug Slavin had nothing to do with it. In fact, he's against it. That's why I thought I'd tell you myself—face to face."

"Five years," Bud said, "the Sox have owned me. And in those five years I've played exactly one half an inning for them. I still think I'm a major-league second baseman."

O'Neill nodded. "So does Jug here. He says that with better breaks you might have been the Sox second baseman long ago. But this is the Blue Sox, Walker, not the South Podunk Beavers. We have a lot of talent to pick and choose from in this organization. I ought to know. I built it."

"Aren't you going to sell me?" Bud asked.

"We tried. But the league seems to be pretty well set at your position. That's another tough break for you. But you know how it is on breaks."

"I ought to," Bud said. "By now anyway."

"Let's not be bitter, Walker. Jug tells me that he gave you the chance to become a utility man five years ago. You turned it down, didn't you?"

"Flat. Yes."

"Why?"

"Because I don't happen to want a permanent career sitting on a bench. I like to play ball. I like to improve, not get rusty in the joints."

O'Neill shrugged. "Well, at least you suited yourself. But now there wouldn't even be that chance left for you. Because on top of all our woes, you've seen fit to create internal dissension. We can't afford to take any of that."

"I don't pick quarrels with anybody. That goes for Devlin, who's the one I guess you're talking about."

"You've picked two with him so far. One in Florida, as soon as you met him. And one yesterday, as soon as you got on the same field with him. Funny, isn't it, that your only quarrels are with the one man who blocked your path?"

"Do you want to hear my side of those quarrels?"

"Not particularly. It doesn't matter who's right and who's wrong in this case. All that matters is that Devlin is our second baseman and you two can't get along. That means one of you has to go, to clear the air, and it can't very well be Devlin, can it?"

"So where do I go from here?"

"Back to Triple-A."

Jug said, "It doesn't have to mean the finish, Walker. If Devlin doesn't hold up, you'll still be my second baseman."

"This is where I came in, five years ago," Bud told him. "But thanks anyway, Mr. Slavin. When do I leave?"

"Tomorrow," O'Neill said. "You don't need to get into uniform today. Just clean out your locker and see Burt Kelly. He's making the arrangements and he'll have your ticket."

O'Neill stood up and then Jug and finally, like a man in a faint daze, Bud got to his feet. He saw O'Neill's extended hand, so he shook it. He saw Jug's, so he shook his too.

As he turned toward the door, he heard Jug say,

"Don't forget, Walker. You still might be back. You never can tell about these things."

He nodded as he walked out, but he thought you really could tell about these things. As he had said to Jug Slavin, this was where he had come in, and it was the same old film with the same old script.

CHAPTER

15

THE OLD SCRIPT INCLUDED A RITUAL BUD REMEMBERED well—cleaning out the locker. He arrived at the locker room early. Out came the glove and the small can of lubricating oil that kept it pliable for the action that he never saw; out came the half-emptied carton of peppermint chewing gum intended to allay the tension that he never got a chance to feel; and out came the cleated shoes, the spare socks, the pictures of his mother and his girl —and the newspaper clippings.

There weren't too many of those, of course. There had been few enough that he had wanted to save. The first one he looked at now was from his home-town paper, dated five years ago. At the time it had been the most exciting clipping of his life. Now it was as depressing as a cold cup of coffee. The headline triumphantly declared, "Blue Sox Sign Local Star."

The story which followed, thanks to the misguided enthusiasm of the local sports editor, indicated that the major leagues would be just about ready to roll over and give up when they got a good look at Second Baseman Bud Walker next spring. At the time he had liked that story, and he had believed it to be true. Now he hated it, because he knew how full of ignorance and false excitement it really was. Such local stories were being written in small-town papers all over the country, week in and week out. And usually they were the last that the baseball world ever heard of the local heroes.

Another little gem was a column written by Ed Daly, known as the Boswell of the Blue Sox, who started out with the team in March and wrote about it until late September. It had been composed the first spring Bud had gone South to the Blue Sox training camp, when nothing seemed to block his path except McNulty. Bud hadn't been alone in thinking so. Ed Daly had thought so too. His printed words proved it.

You can't beat this Sox farm system, believe me. They've got the push buttons which, when pressed, deliver the sound replacement for the guy on his way out. As we all knew then, last year was the third-act curtain on the long and busy career of John McNulty. So, at this crucial moment, what happens? O'Neill pushes the button that brings up a twenty-two-year-old kid named Bud Walker. Walker, it develops, has in his quiet way just about everything a big-league second baseman ought to have, with the possible exception of what my colleagues refer to as color or crowd appeal.

By that I mean this kid Walker doesn't knock you over with 400-foot drives or acrobatics on the field. But he wins you over, when you watch him day after day, by the steady, solid way he plays that bag. He's aggressive. He's a hustler. And he's just about the fastest man on a pivot you'll ever want to see.

He can hit, of course. He probably won't join the upper-bracket boys who club the ball for .300 and better. But he'll hit a hundred points better than his weight, which is around 175, and he's a steadying influence on a pitching staff, because he makes the tough double play. He'll probably never make the All-Star team, because other second basemen will outhit him and out-somersault him. But he'll be around longer than most of those dazzling boys who do make it. And that, in a pecan shell, is as close as I can come to telling you the kind of a second baseman that this kid Walker appears to be.

Bud had always loved Daly for writing that. In the depths of his most discouraged moments, he had pulled that faded clipping out and read it slowly, half aloud, and it had usually helped. But it didn't help now, somehow. It left a bad taste in his mouth.

As he stuffed the clippings with the rest of the locker stuff inside the overnight bag he had brought along, he heard the door open. Pete Gibbs was standing there. Bud had never seen the big catcher arrive so early. It surprised him and dismayed him, too, because he had wanted to clear out, bag and baggage, before any of them got there. He wanted no fraternal farewells. He had a feeling they weren't in order, anyway. The team would all be relieved that he was going, because with his departure one of the big Sox problems would be settled; the dissension would end. He had never really belonged, been one of them. He had been forever an outsider, someone who hung on the fringe a little while and then crawled back to wherever he had come from.

Pete Gibbs walked over to him and said, "I heard you were leaving for a while."

"Quite a while," Bud said. "In fact. . . ."

"That's why I came over early. To catch you."

"Why?"

"Look, Walker," Gibbs said, and his voice sounded almost severe. "I want to tell you something. Dead earnest stuff. You in a mood for the dead earnest stuff?"

"I'm in a mood. It covers anything."

"I know. The whole deal looks black to you right now. It did to me, a year ago. I'm the one guy on this team who knows exactly how you feel, exactly what you're going through."

"I doubt it. That's a bigger statement than you think."

"No, it isn't. Last year they had me heading back to the bushes. Third time and out, too. For keeps. But here it is, a new year, and it looks like I'm first-string catcher for the Sox."

"You are and that's fine. But. . . ."

"Right now you're pretty busy feeling sorry for yourself, Walker, the way I was too. A guy pulled me over the hump then. Name of Tweet Tillman. And I didn't have a prayer to go on. But you. . . . Listen, you've got plenty."

"Like what, for instance?"

"Like this. The team isn't right. The team isn't headed for a pennant; it's headed for the second division. Walker, I know that, because I was with this team last year when they were really headed somewhere. It was all different. Maybe it's impossible to put your finger on it, but it's my theory second base is at the root of it."

"It's apparently not Slavin's theory. Or O'Neill's."

"Don't be too sure about Slavin. O'Neill isn't a ballplayer; he's a corporation, and he thinks in terms of the people who clip coupons, the stockholders. He's got to like Devlin. But I don't think Slavin is mesmerized by the home runs Devlin hits or the acrobatics he pulls off on the field."

"That sounds fine. Great. But he didn't fight to keep me."

"He's in no position to fight on an issue that's a

personal one with O'Neill. Not with us floundering around and you and Devlin acting like a cat and a dog. There's a terrible looseness in this team, and he knows it isn't due to guys like Madigan or Bates or Fiske or Valenti."

"That's swell to hear. Thanks for the inspiration as I hit the old chute. And this time I'm no kid any more, like the last time."

"Well, as a final inspirational word, Walker, the pitchers are the guys who are completely unsold on Devlin. They know he's flashy and they know he's quick. They know it's hard to buck the paying customers, who love him to death. But he doesn't give a pitcher a sense of security as a second baseman should. That's what they tell me, anyway."

"Wish they'd tell Slavin too."

"I think a couple of them have hinted at it."

"And O'Neill."

"Listen, O'Neill is the front office and the front office is what decides how much dough you'll make next year or whether you'll play ball for Gravel City instead of the Sox. You don't make suggestions to the front office, any more than supermarket clerks tell the district manager about the strawberries looking lovely at the top of the box and being all beat up underneath."

"Well, you told me a lot of things. Thanks."

"I told you because I think you're ready to quit.

I was ready to quit when Tweet Tillman told *me* things. I didn't quit and look what happened. Don't quit, Walker. Don't ever quit."

"I won't quit. But if I ever could have a chance. I never had a chance. Just one half of one miserable inning—that's all I ever had."

"You'll get the chance. You know why I think so?"

"No."

"Because Devlin is the kind of a ballplayer who'll beat himself. I'd bet on it."

Bud wouldn't bet on it, but he didn't say so. He liked Pete Gibbs for being friendly and helpful. But what he said, no matter how Bud wished he could believe it, was still just so much inspirational malarkey.

That was what he thought then. A few hours later, though, he thought quite differently.

CHAPTER

16

BEFORE BUD LEFT THE PARK, HE SAW BURT KELLY AND got his one-way ticket to what he thought of as the end of the world. Then he went back to the hotel to leave his bag in the room. There was nothing else to do now until tomorrow morning. And killing time had never been an easy task for him. If he just sat here in the room, there would be nothing to do but brood. That was certainly not the ticket. Movies, somehow, didn't seem to be the answer; he looked over the list in the paper and there wasn't a single one he wanted to see. Finally he went out and just started to walk.

He window-shopped as he strolled. He stopped in a sporting goods store and bought some trout flies for no very good reason that he could think of. Then he headed for a restaurant and ordered a lunch which he left half-eaten on his plate. He started to walk again. He walked with apparent aimlessness but, as it turned out, there was actually nothing aimless about it. When the big concrete facade of the stadium suddenly loomed in front of him, he knew that this was where he had been headed all the time, as directly as an arrow aimed at a target.

It was almost game time. He went to the players' entrance where, for a change, the little gray-headed man who tended the gate had no trouble at all in identifying him.

"Better hurry up, Walker," he said. "You haven't got much time left."

"I keep bankers' hours," Bud told him.

He didn't follow the tunnel to the dressing room today. He made for the first-base side of the stadium and turned up one of the ramps. Walking out into the bright sunlight was like emerging from a cave. He chose a seat high up in the unreserved grandstand section, slightly beyond first base, bought a bag of peanuts, and settled back for a busman's holiday.

The crowd was small, even for a weekday afternoon, because the Sox had lost five straight now. If they didn't salvage this final game of the Redskin series, the roof would really cave in on them. But they had Lasky pitching and they always looked a little cocky, no matter what, when Lasky was on the mound.

He mowed down the first three Redskin hitters in order, with only one ball going to the outfield.

The Sox trooped in and Madigan strode up to the plate.

Madigan was a perfect lead-off man. He didn't hit above .260 over the course of a season, but he knew how to make a pitcher expend the limit of energy to get him. He managed to reach first base through a walk or an error or some convenient fluke as often as by a clean base hit. And he led the league every year in getting hit in harmless parts of his body by pitched balls, with such regularity that some people suspected it was not a mere coincidence.

The Redskin pitcher today was Bob Avery, who had not acquired the nickname of Robert the Rip on the strength of his slow ball. When Avery saw Madigan digging in for a toe hold, he blazed an inside pitch that was designed to loosen him up and make him think twice before digging in again. But Madigan merely spun away from the path of Avery's fireball and promptly took another toe hold.

Avery caught the outside corner, but Madigan didn't stir. He threw another ball, and then another strike, and still Madigan did not move the bat from his shoulder. It was two and two now, and Avery rifled the next one in. Madigan swung late and fouled it off. Avery rifled another one in. Madigan fouled it again. A trifle discouraged at Madigan's ability to spoil his prize pitch so easily, Avery tried his change-up and missed the corner. So Madigan, as he did so often, had run the count to three and two and had already forced Avery to make seven careful pitches.

Avery's eighth pitch was another one right out of the slingshot and Madigan did not deign to accept the challenge of its cocky speed. He did not really swing at it. He merely pushed his bat at it and met it evenly. It was the force of Avery's arm, not Madigan's bat, which sent it looping into right field for an anemic-looking single, but a single, none the less.

Madigan danced insolently off the bag as the Redskin infield crept in a little, looking for the bunt. Chip Fiske gave it to them neatly on the third pitch. It trickled down the third-base line and though Fiske was nailed, Madigan arrived without incident at second.

Valenti now stepped in and did not hesitate any more than a small boy with a quarter in his pocket facing a candy-store window. He took a cut, full and hard, at the very first pitch. Again it was Robert the Rip's ripper. The ball shot toward center, rising as it went, and a yell rose from the stands, too.

However, in straightaway centerfield, where this ball sailed, was a long, endless pocket of green. The Redskin center fielder had played Valenti correctly, and he was fleet of foot. He caught it with a high flick of his glove near the extreme barrier, while the crowd gasped its dismay. Madigan, who had returned to the bag when he saw that the catch was going to be made, tagged up and jogged into third standing up.

Now Blake, slinging two bats behind him as he entered the box, faced Avery. The crowd unleashed eager howls of anticipation. All they wanted from the powerful Beef Trust this time was a measly single. But Avery had other notions. He fed Blake outside stuff—not pitch-outs, but teasers designed to induce Blake to swing at pitches he could not hit solidly. But Blake didn't go after them and soon trotted down to first as the crowd booed Avery.

Kennie Willard followed Blake. Suddenly Avery couldn't find the strike zone, now that he wanted to. Only one pitch out of five to Willard came in, and he too moved down to first, while Blake advanced to second. Madigan was dancing impatiently on third as Devlin strode up with the bases full and the crowd roaring their confidence in him.

Devlin was not one to fade when the spotlight burned brightly upon him. He took a ball, fouled off a strike, and then he found a pitch to his liking —Robert the Rip's fastest fast ball. His line drive whistled furiously over the shortstop's head into left center. It was a sure single and most likely a double.

Bud watched Devlin the way he always watched him, like a camera trained to miss nothing. Devlin, charging down the base line, did not have his head down like a runner. He had it craned up and out, to his left. The flight of his hit was a pretty thing to watch and Devlin apparently did not wish to miss any of it. That meant, of course, that he was not moving with the last ounce of speed in his legs.

He rounded first and kept on going. All three Sox runners were flying toward home. No one tried to nip them. The throw came in to second, and it reached the bag just barely ahead of Devlin. The tag got him. His hit had driven in two runs, but the third runner didn't score, because Devlin had made the third out before the runner crossed the plate.

There was Devlin for you, Bud thought angrily. He had driven in two runs, of course, so he was a hero. But he had thrown away a third run and probably more, for the rally that had been alive a moment ago was dead now. Avery had been on the ropes. One more hit or walk would have put him out of there. Now, however, he could retire to the shade of the dugout to cool off and calm his frayed nerves, with the possibility of coming back refreshed and as strong as a bull again.

The crowd still roared their delight with Devlin as he went out to the grass back of second to pick up his glove. They kept applauding him, so he tipped his cap as he trotted out, and made them happy. He had thrown away a run and choked off a rally, and no one would know until the ninth how much he had hurt his team's cause. And if the Sox lost the game, no one would remember. They would only remember that he had come through in the clutch and driven in the first Sox runs.

He brought them to their feet again in the top of the third when he dashed madly into right field after a short, tricky fly. It was by all rights too deep for him, but Fiske could not yell him off of it. At the last second Fiske ducked and let Devlin grab it, and the crowd really went wild. So did Fiske, but in a slightly different way. Even from the upper reaches of the grandstand, Bud could tell that Fiske was bawling Devlin out. Devlin just stared at him and then returned to his position, tipping his cap again to the crowd's applause. In far right field, the bleachers let loose with a sudden wave of boos, and Fiske couldn't have had any illusions about where they were directed. As far as the crowd was concerned, anyone who tangled with Devlin was automatically in error. Their boy could do no wrong.

Avery had settled down ominously after his rocky start, as so often happens. Given the kind of a break that Avery had been given by Devlin, the pitcher who was ready for the showers in the first inning frequently returns to the wars in an invincible mood. That was what Avery had done now.

The innings crept by. Lasky was his usual tough self today, but not quite tough enough to make two runs stand up. The Redskins got to him for one in the fifth and another in the eighth. The ninth was scoreless for both sides and they went in to the tenth all tied up at 2-2.

Then, with the first two batters disposed of, Lasky gave up a single and a walk. A slow roller went down toward second, and when Devlin's snap throw missed by a flick, the bases were loaded. Lasky began to pitch with the worried deliberateness of a man scaling a cliff. His first offering was greeted by a swinging strike. His second was high. His third was high, too, but the fourth pitch was in there, and the batter swung.

He swung under it. It squirted up in the air, not deep or hard, but aimed toward the no man's land between second base and right field. Devlin was after it like the streak that he was, and the crowd rose to their feet and screamed encouragement. He was not one to let his public down. Fiske was plunging in and yelling Devlin away, but Devlin kept racing, knowing that Fiske had always ducked in time. If it fell in, it was a three-run pop fly, because all runners had been off with the swing.

Devlin didn't slacken; Fiske didn't slacken. The ball came down, and they were both there, and this time Fiske didn't duck. Two trains meeting head on never took each other off the tracks more cleanly. In the next instant both men were stretched on the ground, and the ball was bouncing crazily with

Valenti in mad pursuit. Valenti got it finally, but the three runs crossed the plate and the batter wound up on second.

Players streamed toward right field. Fiske was getting up slowly, looking dazed. Devlin was still lying there. Then the circle of players hid them both, but when Bud saw the stretcher being raced out, he knew it wasn't for Fiske.

Devlin lay on it, motionless, as they carried him off amidst the dead silence of the crowd. Bud put his hand in his pocket and felt the little envelope with the one-way ticket inside. The final thing that Pete Gibbs had said to him in the locker room rushed into his mind. "Devlin," Gibbs had said, "is the kind of a ballplayer who'll beat himself. I'd bet on it."

Well, maybe Devlin hadn't entirely beaten himself, but this had all the earmarks of a reprieve for Bud Walker. And no matter how short a reprieve it might be, it would still be that chance that he had failed for so many years to get.

CHAPTER

17

THE CLUBHOUSE WAS EMPTY. BUD HAD NO LOCKER as yet, having given his up yesterday. He would have one again pretty quickly now, no doubt about that, but for the moment he was a stray. He sat down on a bench, opened his overnight bag, and took out his glove and the small can of oil. He began to oil the deep pocket of the glove with more enthusiasm than he had felt in quite a while. This time he was oiling it for action. This was the real thing.

Jug's phone call last night had been just like him, short and to the point. He had said, "Walker, don't use that train ticket tomorrow."

"No?"

"No. Show up at the clubhouse early. Around noon. You know why. I'll be there. You play tomorrow."

"I'm ready," he had said.

He certainly was. The reason why he was going to play today wasn't very flattering, but he had reached the point where that didn't matter. Just the chance to play was enough. Plenty.

His eyes narrowed to thoughtful slits as he rubbed the oil around and around in the well of the glove, working methodically and with diligence. He liked this job when there was a reason for it. It seemed hard to believe that after all these years the one big chance he had sweated for so long was finally here. He thought dimly of all the ball clubs he had labored for in the past seven years; they were enough to crisscross a map of the United States.

The locker room door opened and Burt Kelly, the road secretary, stuck his head in. His red, cherubic face showed signs of vast relief when he spotted Bud. He waddled over, a caricature of a fashion advertisement for the pin-striped double-breasted suit. Kelly always looked overheated and overworked, as though he needed to mop his brow but lacked the energy.

"Well, Walker!" he said, as though stumbling over Bud here was as big a surprise as bumping into General MacArthur in the right-field bleachers. "The best-laid plans of mice and men and all that. Well, well! Got the ticket on you?"

"Got it," Bud said.

He pulled it out of his pocket and Kelly stuffed it in a wallet that looked big enough to hold a road map.

"Need this," Kelly explained. "Got to turn it in. Have to account for everything on this job."

"I'll bet," Bud said.

"Got here early, I see," Kelly said.

"Sure did."

"Got a break. Wish you luck."

"May need it," Bud told him, wondering just how long you had to be around Burt Kelly before you acquired his proficiency in speaking the English language without the use of the personal pronoun.

Kelly left. Bud kept on oiling the glove.

The door opened again after a while, and this time Jug Slavin entered. Even in street clothes, the Sox manager looked every inch the ballplayer, from his seamy, sun-wrinkled face to his oversized hands. He planted one foot on the bench and thrust his long jaw close to Bud as he spoke, a habit no doubt picked up through all those years of baiting umpires at close range.

"A month," Jug said. "Doc Dougherty says he'll be out that long at least."

"Shoulder? Head?"

"The elbow. A chip has to be removed. It means an operation."

"What about Fiske?"

"Fiske is O.K. Personally, I think Fiske let him have it. But you never know. Anyway, I can finally confirm what I've told you twice—five years ago and this March. You're my second baseman. But don't get too excited; it's on a very temporary basis."

"I know."

"When Devlin comes back, he's back. The statistics say that, the crowd says that—and O'Neill says that."

"Sure."

"To tell you the truth, Walker, I don't hold out much hope for you, no matter what. It's only fair to tell you that. Not that you don't know it anyway."

"I'm not as sure about it as you are."

"Well, don't quit hoping. But what with the club's investment in Devlin and the magnet he is at the box office, you're up against the toughest odds I've ever seen. Just so you know it."

"Which I do."

"And don't expect any enthusiastic welcome from the crowd. Anybody taking Devlin's place is bound to be a bum in their eyes. Get yourself set for that."

"I'm set."

"You're a sound ballplayer, Walker. You just go ahead, do your best, and don't think about a month from now. Just think about today's ball game."

"Yeah."

"Well, that's about all. You'll bat eighth. Bates will be back today, so you'll be working alongside of a real pro. Pay no attention to the fans. Keep your chin up. And hustle every minute."

"Nobody has to tell me to hustle, Mr. Slavin."

"No, I know that. But even so . . . well . . . I hate to paint a gloomy picture, Walker, but I like to give my ballplayers the straight dope. And yours is a definitely gloomy picture—in terms of one month from now."

CHAPTER

18

WHEN THE TEAM SPRANG OUT OF THE DUGOUT, TROT-
ting to their positions to start the opening game
of this series with the Panthers, the routine cheer
from the stands was as feeble as a defective peanut
whistle. Anyone listening closely might have heard
a few scattered boos in the background, too.

That was hardly surprising, Bud thought. The
team had dropped six straight now. The fans' fair-
haired boy was out indefinitely, and in his place
was somebody named Walker, a guy who would
already have been back where he belonged in the
minors except for an accident. So far there had
been nothing for them to cheer about this season
except Devlin. Now Devlin had been taken away
from them. Theirs was a mood of gloom and surly
pessimism.

Chip Fiske caught up with Bud. Chip said,
"Don't worry about the crowd if they get on you.
They probably will. And on me, too."

Bud nodded and grunted. Let him make a single

mistake and they'd be on him, all right. He could
see that coming. The thing to do was to make no
mistakes and keep making no mistakes. Other rookies could and they could get away with it. But not
Devlin's replacement.

Bix Hanson was pitching today. He hadn't
pitched a really good game this year. He hadn't
found last year's looseness or last year's stuff. He
was developing the deadly habit of pitching a ball
game with one eye on the bull pen. Bud watched
him finish his warm-up tosses and then look around
with the worried frown that seemed to crease the
foreheads of most Sox pitchers these days.

Bix looked at Pete Gibbs, in the crouch now as
the Panther lead-off man got set. Bud, too, looked
at Pete and from his fielding position he caught the
signal. The fast ball. Bud took a slight step backward as Bix toed the rubber.

"Number one now, Bix," he called.

"Let's get him, Bix boy," Patsy Bates yelled.

"The easy one, Bix, the easy one," Madigan
shouted.

Bud saw Bix's big arm come up and around. He
saw the ball turn into a white blur, then hit Pete's
mitt with explosive force as the Panther lead-off
man swung hard but late.

A strike on the first pitch always brings the crowd
to life. But this one didn't. They sat in silence. Bix

threw again. Another fast streak, though lower—just above the knees. The hitter swung. He swung so hard he lost his balance and went down in the dirt. The crowd stirred at this. But not too much.

Bix missed the corner with a couple of curves. Then he put one in there. The batter swung and topped it. The ball glanced off his bat and trickled between third and the mound. Bix pounced on it but he betrayed his tenseness: he had to make two grabs at it before he picked it up. When he finally threw, his throw was wide and Blake's foot came off the bag. The Panther was on.

Now the crowd came to life, with a groan of pain and disgust.

Bix looked tense and he was: he walked the next man. Out in the bull pen the baseballs began to fly back and forth. It was almost routine this year, that quick activity in the Sox bull pen.

The third Panther hitter took two balls and then tried to bunt, to move the runners along to second and third. Bix refused to let him see anything too good, and as result he lost him entirely. That filled the bases and brought Gibbs out to the mound for a chat. Madigan walked over to join them. So did Bates and Bud.

"No hurry, Bix," Madigan said. "Plenty of time."

"Just don't give this guy anything fat," Gibbs said, "or he'll cut one of Madigan's legs off with it."

"Every pitch low," Bix said.

Gibbs nodded, and they all went back to their positions.

They knew that a solid blow now would really put Bix on the ropes. This had been happening too often. It was the pattern that was beating them day after day. If only Bix could get out of this jam, he might settle down and pitch a fine game. But it was a big if.

Bix shaded a corner of the plate with his first pitch and got it by for a called strike. He threw a wide one at the knees for a ball. Then he shook Gibbs off with a nervous twitch of the head, and Bud saw Gibbs calling for the knuckler.

It fluttered toward the plate, but it fell outside and low and that made it two balls and one strike. The next one, thought Bud, had better be in there or else the fat pitch would follow.

"Way ahead, Bix," he yelled. "Way ahead."

It went in, medium fast and low. The batter slashed. The ball went toward Bates, hopping wickedly and without enough speed to look like a sure double-play ball. Bates played it for the hop he wanted and snapped it toward Bud at the bag. Bud grabbed it and knew by instinct that the odds now favored the batter's race to first. As Bud touched the bag he was aware, without a time-wasting glance, that the charging runner was coming into him with a football block, to take him out.

Up he shot, straight into the air, and in the same moment he got the throw off, snapping it hard and straight toward Blake's waiting mitt. As he came down, clear of the runner but letting him have a good look at his spikes, he saw the first-base umpire's right thumb jerk up and heard the crowd's quick, joyful roar.

A run had scored, but the threat of the big inning had been all but wiped away. Relief was apparent in Bix's face. The worried crease was gone now. One run was in, to be sure, but there were two outs now and just a single runner left, on third. Bix looked loose and cool and acted it, getting the third out on a swinging strike. Bud skimmed his glove behind him with the unerring aim that had become a habit, making it land just a foot or two on the grass. Then he trotted to the dugout.

The crowd was applauding. But it was not for him. It was for Bix. As they saw it, good pitching had pulled the team out of the jam; the double play had been an automatic thing because Bix had pitched right.

Bix touched his cap to them as he stepped into the dugout, but when Bud followed him, he slapped him on the arm and said, "I never thought it was a D.P. ball, kid. Now I feel like a million."

"A swifty, this Walker," Bates said.

Bud grinned his pleasure. If the fans couldn't see

the difference between that play and Devlin's . . . well, Bix did and so did Bates.

Jug Slavin moved over and said to Bix, "Feel O.K.?"

"I feel fine," Bix said. "Why shouldn't I? Getting that D.P. was like cashing in an insurance policy."

The Sox, however, were one run behind and finding it difficult to even things up. Klavansky, who was pitching for the Panthers, was a real ace, though it was hard to figure out exactly why, because he didn't throw much of anything except fast balls. Still, he was a tough proposition.

Madigan popped up. Fiske struck out, and took a fine flurry of boos from the crowd. Valenti grounded sharply to third. That was that. But the first inning had been a tonic to Bix. He set the Panthers down in order on seven pitched balls. It was in the last of the second that Bud made his first trip to the plate and got a real taste of how the crowd felt about him.

There were Sox runners on first and third with two out when he stepped in, and the crowd gave him a groan, just to let him know where he stood as a hitter in their estimation. He ran the count to three and two and then hit one solidly, but it was a line drive straight at the shortstop, who picked it off his shoulder for the final out. As Bud rounded first and headed out to pick up his glove, the fans behind first base opened up on him.

"Nice clutch hit, kid!"

"Guess you know why they never gave *you* a bonus, Walker."

"Was that your long ball, busher?"

He kicked an imaginary pebble but he didn't look their way. The game settled down, with Bix and Klavansky locked in a tight duel. Nothing, absolutely nothing, happened. It was still 1-0 for the Panthers when the Sox came in to bat in the last of the eighth, and Jug Slavin was giving off sparks.

"What is this?" he demanded of the whole dugout. "First well-pitched game we get this year and we can't even make a run to back it up. This Klavansky doesn't throw a thing except that fast ball. Hardly ever a curve. What's he got that keeps you big sluggers looking like banjo players?"

"Skipper," Madigan said, "that ball of Klavansky's gets right up to you and then it ducks in on you. Or it does something. It's not exactly straight the way it looks."

"Well, it must do something, because we don't do anything," Jug snapped. "And we better begin now."

Fiske was up, and Fiske singled. Valenti bunted him to second. Blake stepped in, and Klavansky looked at him in the tired, unhappy way of fast-ball pitchers in the late innings, especially when they face the power boys. Klavansky turned, glanced toward left field and center field, and wiped his hand across his glistening forehead.

Blake settled his huge body firmly in the box and waited, chewing rhythmically on the huge wad of gum that always bulged his cheek. Klavansky stretched both hands high, dropped them to his belt, and settled his shoulders. He rocked. He threw. And Blake swung. The smash was solid. The ball soared deep to left above the frantically racing left fielder and it dropped, finally, into the bleachers. Blake jogged around behind Fiske and when he reached the dugout, Slavin was on the step. Blake said, "You were right, Skip."

"About what?" Slavin said.

"Klavansky. He don't pitch nothing but straight balls. You should have told me sooner. I could have got those runs for Bix any time if you had only told me, Skip."

Then in the top of the ninth, with his one-run lead, Bix started to wobble for the second time in the game. He, too, was tiring. He got the first man, but Blake booted a grounder. Then a fluttering-quail type of pop-fly single to left, followed by a walk, filled the bases with only one out.

Bix pitched low and got in the hole, two and nothing. He finally came in with the third one and it was hit, deep and hard, between third and short. It looked like a two-run single and the ball game when it started out. But it wasn't. Bates, somehow, got there with his octopus-like spread of arms. He flipped furiously to Bud. Bud took it at the bag, shot high into the air above the runner trying to give him the take-out slide, and snapped it on to Blake. It got there and that was the ball game.

The crowd was roaring as they trooped in, but again there was no applause for Bud. It was for Bates, and Bates alone. Bud could not help but wonder if it occurred to the crowd that both the double plays in which he had been the pivot man could hardly have been pulled off by Devlin, and that without both, the Panthers would have had far more runs than they needed.

But he knew the crowd was not thinking along those lines. Just as he ducked into the tunnel entrance, a fan hooted, "Good day, huh, Walker? None out of four! You slugger!"

That was how it was and that was how it would stay. He might as well get used to it. But the main thing was, the Sox had snapped that losing streak —with him, not Devlin, playing second base.

CHAPTER
19

FAST MAN ON A PIVOT   143

'THE SOX HAD FINALLY PICKED THEMSELVES OFF THE floor in that first game with the Panthers. They soon proved it. They swept the series and took two out of three in each of the next two series, and that was winning ball.

It meant that they finished the home stand against the Western clubs on the upbeat, even though their over-all record for it showed only seven wins against five losses. That, in itself, didn't look too impressive. But the important fact to Bud, although it seemed to escape everyone else's notice, was that three of those five games in the lost column had been played with Devlin at second base. The record after his enforced departure was seven wins against only two losses. That was something, Bud thought.

But who else thought so? No one, as far as he knew. The home crowd did not warm to him; and the sportswriters who, in the long run, molded their opinions for them, failed to point out any connection

between the second-base switch and the team's up-
surge.

This was a sample of press opinion.

The Blue Sox have now managed to edge into the
first division as they take off for the West. But
they've been pretty lucky to do it and they'll have
to keep on being pretty lucky to hold their place,
much less move up, because they show a deficit in
power and they've been winning their games by the
skin of their teeth. Their victories have been low-
score contests gained by one and two-run margins.
The Sox pitchers can't stand that sort of strain very
long. No staff of pitchers could.

The answer? Well, mostly Devlin. Before his
temporary retirement he was banging the ball at a
.330 clip and covering more territory than a gazelle.
In fact, it was his ability to cover more territory
than most second basemen that put him on the
shelf.

And in his place what do we have? A veteran
rookie named Bud Walker who already had a train
ticket to the minors in his hand when the accident
befell Devlin. Walker, in his brief sojourn at second
base, is hitting a miserable .227—one hundred points
below the Comet—and he does not produce that
long ball as Devlin does. Going by the records, you
might say that the Sox have been winning more
consistently since Devlin left the line-up, and that's
true. But the point, as this reporter sees it, is that

only lately have the jittery Sox pitchers started to find themselves. If they had been pitching this sort of ball when Devlin was in there, our boys would undoubtedly be on top of the heap instead of clinging to the fourth rung of the ladder. It's a weak-looking Sox team with the punchless Walker in there and let's hope our boys can manage to hold the fort somehow until the fleet Comet gets back in action.

There it was, Bud thought, all wrapped up in a package for you. What the man said sounded like logic. Anybody who read it would no doubt nod and murmur assent. All it overlooked in its logic, of course, was that it was Walker's steadiness at second that had made the pitchers steady. And that Devlin's flashy unsteadiness would make them jittery all over again.

Bud's weak hitting, however, bothered him plenty. He was hitting way below what he knew to be his best and he knew why. It was the pressure —the straining to hit over his head and diminish the gap between Devlin's power and his own. He would not have felt that pressure, he was sure, if he were certain of his job instead of aware that the time was short and the odds against him heavy, and that he would have to produce very soon in order to prove anything.

There were those, however, who found something

good to say about him. Some of the reporters noticed little things about the way he played ball that deserved notice. Bud had saved one such clipping, an interview with the Panther manager, who said about the Sox:

"They're bound to miss a great all-around second baseman like Shore, of course. I haven't seen their new star, Devlin, but this fill-in, Walker, is a pleasure to watch from a managerial standpoint, just because of the way he goes down that line after he hits a ball. It always kills me to see the number of big-league players who run down to first watching the flight of the ball and taking a final peek at it just before it reaches the bag.

"This boy Walker really hustles every time. It shows me the type of ballplayer he is. His primary interest is in stretching the hit to the limit of its possibilities. Watch him sometime as he rounds first base. Watch exactly how he does it. Notice that he always pivots on the bag with his left foot, never his right. That gives him the turn on the inside and saves him maybe a full step if he's going for second. He must have trained himself hard for that, because not too many ballplayers are able to do it or are ambitious enough to learn to do it.

"And another thing. The only hit he got against us in the whole series that was better than a single would have been no more than a single with most ballplayers. Did he take his turn at first base the way most of them do? No. Most of them go about ten feet past the bag before they return to it. Not Walker. He went about twenty-five feet toward second base on what looked like just a routine single. By going that distance, he was close enough to second to judge accurately and instantly whether he could beat a throw to the bag if there were any sloppy handling of his hit in the outfield. That time it did happen to be handled sloppily and he kept going and made it, for a double. That is not reckless running; that is smart, heads-up running."

Then, during the following series with the Bears, one of their coaches had been asked by a reporter how this year's edition of the Sox looked to him. And from that interview Bud got his second—and last—note of appreciation. Funny, he thought. The kind words come only from the opposition, not from the home front.

This coach said:

"I've heard a lot of moaning since I hit this town about how crippled the Sox are with a journeyman second baseman like Walker filling Shore's big gap. Well, Walker hasn't made a single hit against us in this series and yet he's impressed me. Some of those double plays he gets in the middle of don't look to be double plays when they start out. And, on the offensive side, it was Walker who beat us in that first game, even though he went four for nothing.

"How? I'll tell you. You remember the score was all tied up in the seventh inning. Walker was on first base after forcing Gibbs at second for the second out of the inning. Eddie Lasky came up, and he must have given Walker the signal to go on the second pitch. Because Walker, who isn't the fastest base runner I ever saw, got a terrific jump on the pitch. He was more than halfway to second when Lasky swung and hit on a line toward right center. Our boy in center, George Wettling, is on the solid side as center fielders go. He had to hustle to block that ball of Lasky's from scooting through for extra bases. His only chance for a play of any kind was a throw to second base to hold Lasky at first.

"Now Walker, because of his great start, was almost to third base before Wettling could get his hands on the ball. So, instead of pulling up at third as a man on first always does on a hit-and-run single, Walker's great jumping start gave him a chance to keep going. He kept going and made it. He actually scored the tie-breaking run all the way from first base on a single and there was no sloppy fielding that helped him do it. He simply ran the bases so skillfully and with so much hustle that no possible defense could have prevented it. The fact that the Sox went on to score three more runs that inning and wrap up the game is, I guess, the reason why nobody seems to have given credit to Walker for really winning the ball game."

Praise like that was rare and good to hear. Bud wondered to what extent Jug Slavin was aware of his contributions to the team's success. He wondered if Slavin looked beyond his anemic batting average. Most likely not. Anyway, Slavin's mind was shut against him as anything except a temporary stopgap, because O'Neill's mind was shut against him.

But even appreciation from the opposition was something to keep him going and he was eager to face the West, eager to get away from the hostility and contempt of the home crowd. If the team kept on winning, they couldn't laugh him off. When Devlin came back and took over, they couldn't say Walker had hurt the team even if they didn't believe he had helped it.

CHAPTER

20

THE BLUE SOX' WINNING WAYS DID NOT END IN THE West; the pattern that had formed during the home stand held firm. To be sure, there wasn't a lot of hitting. Few games were settled by a margin of more than a few runs. But the team had drive and hustle and the pitching remained superb. Even the reporters who had been full of misgivings at the start, predicting a catastrophic nose dive, began to look at the Sox with a new curiosity and hope. "The Sox bull pen," one of them wrote, "has become a place where men take slow sun baths and stir no more than checker players in the village general store."

The Sox paid the Redskins back for that humiliating sweep scored over them earlier in the season at home. They did not quite pay them in full, but they took two out of three. Then they split a brief two-game series with the Panthers, whose third-place berth they were trying to take over. And they took it over when they moved on and swept the

apathetic Bears three times in three games. They
wound up their swing with just a split in the two-
game joust with the Hawks, but it meant that they
headed East with a road record of seven won and
three lost. They had climbed over the shoulders of
the sagging Panthers and were only a game and a
half behind the second-place Redskins and three
games behind the pace-setting Clippers.

On the train for the East the reporters asked Jug
Slavin to explain what had got into this outfit, which
had looked for a while like the poorest Sox team in
years. Bud read his answer in the papers two days
later. Jug was quoted as saying:

> "I don't know how to put my finger on it exactly.
> I don't think it's any one thing. It's a lot of things
> and a lot of guys, and they're all pulling together
> the way they weren't at first. It takes a little time,
> you know, to get twenty-five men of different tem-
> peraments working in one groove, with one idea in
> mind. That's a manager's job and it's not always
> easy to get them all thinking your way and doing
> things the way you feel they should be done. They
> all have ideas of their own, but once they get the
> thought that only one way is the right one, that's
> when you have a ball club.
>
> "This Sox surge is not, I think, the work of any
> one man or couple of men. It's everybody pitching
> in and thinking they can win and going out and
> hustling for it, without jealousies and friction. This

team caught a good fever some way or other. They are not aiming for fourth place or third place or second place. They've got nothing in mind but the pennant.

"They're winning the games the right way—close, hard, and with hustle. They aren't looking at the scoreboard and wondering how somebody else is doing. They are going after each little game, and never mind what's happening elsewhere.

"We need more hitting than this team has been doing and usually we get it from our batting order. But Blake has been in a mild slump and of course Devlin was quite a thump when he was in there, while Walker is . . . well . . . hitting .227. In fairness to Walker, I must say he's a steady man in the field and has been great on those double-play pivots that pull the pitchers out of the serious jams. With the kind of pitching we're getting now and the added wallop of Devlin, we'll be up there where we belong in due time."

Even faint praise from Jug was pleasant, but of course he had made it clear enough that Walker was no serious threat to Devlin. If Jug thought there was any connection between Walker and the good pitching he was getting, he had not indicated it.

Bud knew his light hitting so far was no true measure of his ability at the plate. He was not the first ballplayer whose hitting had suffered from the lack of a sense of security. If he had that second-base job outright, he knew he would loosen up. He was thankful, at least, that his poor hitting hadn't bogged down his fielding, as so often happened to ballplayers in a batting slump.

The Western trip had been full of interest to him in many ways. It was the first time he had ever traveled with the big-leaguers, lived with them, and had a taste of what the life was like. He saw already that a big-league ball club was like no other group in the world, in or out of sports. In this setup, kids barely out of their teens and men pushing forty shared equally in the responsibility for the club's success. Where else would you find an organization with such a structure?

Then, too, Bud had not fully realized before how odd it was that in such an organization a young unknown making six or seven thousand a year might be doing more for the team than the big star making fifty thousand. That didn't usually make sense in terms of anything else in the world, but it frequently made sense on a big-league ball club.

He had a chance to observe the strangely assorted people living together. For instance, the Sox had a young pitcher they were grooming, via the bull pen, for later stardom. His name was Roger Brentano and he was two years out of Harvard with a master's degree in English literature. He roomed with Turk Pavone, who was not too many years out of the Marine Corps by way of Third Avenue, New York,

and said he vaguely remembered the seventh grade
but nothing beyond that. When these two room-
mates spent an evening together in the hotel, Roger
read Chaucer and Turk read comic books. But they
got along fine.

Then, on all clubs there were two kinds of men:
the ones who were full of fast talk and personality
and had an easy way with other people, and the
"loners" who liked to be by themselves and seldom
talked much. Throwing them together on a full-
time basis was sometimes a funny business.

Bud often thought that the fans who really believed, as many did, that it took a rah-rah spirit like
that of a college team to win a pennant, would be
shocked to look behind the scenes at the Blue Sox,
champions from way back, and see their heroes
taking life easy off the field.

Fans, he knew, thought the players were a tight
band who stuck together like hornets inside a nest,
twenty-fours hours a day. Nothing could have been
further from the truth. When they finished a game,
the chances usually were that most of them would
not even see each other until the next day in the
locker room, just before batting practice.

They were not even in the habit of eating together except on trains, where they had to. When
they went to the movies it was usually in pairs, not
in groups. When they played cards, each was in-
clined to stick to his own little more or less perma-

nent group. The married men usually numbered their best friends among people outside of the baseball world and, unlike fellow workers in an office, seldom got together socially. On the road trips most of the men who had been around for years renewed acquaintance with friends in every town. The young fellows who did not know the ground so well spent their time at the movies or playing pinball games or pool.

The only basic interest that the group of twenty-five players who comprise a big-league squad actually had in common was the hope of winning today's ball game and this year's pennant. There it began and there it ended. During the course of their careers, so many of them were shifted around from team to team by trade and sale that the ties of the team were far from binding.

Until now Bud had never had thought of it that way. He had thought of the players as a band, tight and close and always together. But that was not how it was.

Before returning to the Blue Sox stadium, the team had two series to play with Eastern rivals in their own ball parks—one with the Chiefs and one with the Grays. Then they would go home for the big one with the visiting Clippers. The Clippers had made them look pretty bad the last time they met, and this series, whether they liked the idea or not, would be a test of their pennant potentialities. If they lost it, their prospects would fade almost to the point of extinction. So there would be heavy pressure on them during the coming encounter with the Clippers.

The Sox took two out of two from the Chiefs. They took three out of three from the Grays. Those five wins, added to their final victory over the Hawks before leaving the West, put them in possession of a healthy six-game winning streak as they took the train for home.

Bud was thinking on the way home that maybe the club's success might have changed the minds of some of the people who governed his destiny. If they needed still more evidence of his usefulness to the club, perhaps he would still have time to provide it before Devlin was ready to come back. But next morning, when he saw the headline on the sports page, his hopes were dashed. It said, "Sox Home, Devlin Ready to Rejoin Them."

The story went on to report that Devlin had been working out daily this last week at the stadium and that the club physician said Devlin had recovered amazingly fast from what he described as an elbow fracture.

"He'll be ready sooner than I thought," Dr. Dougherty was quoted as saying. "In fact, he might be ready for this Clipper series—for pinch-hitting at least."

Bingo, Bud thought. That's what they really ought to nickname him. Bingo Devlin. He sure draws the right numbers.

CHAPTER

21

JUG SLAVIN WAS THE TYPE OF MANAGER WHO HAS A deep respect for the hungry ballplayer, since he had been one himself. He knew what it was to come up the hard way. In his early days he had been tagged "No Prospect" by many scouts, because he had been a hulk of a kid, slow to catch on to things, and awkward in action. He had plugged through more minor-league years than he cared to remember, but he had emerged finally as a big-league shortstop—a man who could think quickly on his feet, deliver the hit under pressure, and look fairly graceful in pursuit of a skipping ground ball.

This background tended to make him suspect people to whom brilliance came easily. He had therefore never been able to shake his feeling of distrust toward Devlin, though he liked brilliance in his ballplayers and Devlin positively had it. With both fans and front office mad about the bonus kid, Slavin would have been a fool to give preference to Walker, whom he liked for special reasons that only an old pro could fully understand. Besides, Slavin had a one-year contract at a fat price, and he also had five children. He had to follow his head, not his emotions.

Yet the way his team had performed since Walker had been a part of it both pleased and disturbed him. He was naturally pleased to see the team function smoothly and successfully. He was disturbed by the feeling that he would inevitably have to shelve a man who might turn out to be that very rare specimen, a key ballplayer—the type who never sets the league afire, or makes the headlines or the All-Star teams, but who serves as the cement that keeps a ball club all in one piece.

What had happened since Walker had taken over second base gave point to his feeling that this man might be just such a key player. Walker's personal record was unimpressive, not to say drab, yet he seemed to give the team something vital. But if Slavin stuck his neck out and gambled on Walker over Devlin, his own job would hang by a thread. On the other hand, he had nothing to lose if he took a gamble on Devlin, the people's choice.

He knew that O'Neill, for very good reasons of his own, was most anxious to get rid of Walker and give a clear field to Devlin. He had already done that before Devlin was injured. He knew also that the fans, who paid for what it cost to build this team, wanted no part of Walker. And yet, as he came close to the day when he would have to make the inevitable decision, he felt an overwhelming reluctance to take Walker out of the line-up.

Jug sat now, in a state of mental weariness, in his small private office at the stadium, many hours before the start of this first game in a series with the Clippers already being referred to as crucial. The league records said Devlin was the man; the fans said it; the front office said it. Yet there was something about Walker as a ballplayer which touched his feelings and stirred his imagination. He couldn't put his finger on what it was, but it was there. He couldn't quite shake it.

As he sat there sipping a cold coke, he rubbed the back of his hand across his forehead in the same way he had always done on the field in his active days as shortstop when the pressure was heavy. He had been unable to eat a decent breakfast, which for him indicated real mental stress. And with a team going along at the fine clip the Sox were going, he should have no reason for mental stress.

It was not surprising that Walker was so much on his mind. The first thing that had happened on Jug's return to town was that O'Neill had phoned him, urging him to get Devlin back into the line-up the first possible day. He hadn't ventured to tell O'Neill that he didn't really want to take Walker out. He knew what a going-over O'Neill would give him if he did. But the feeling persisted that here, after many years, a genuine big-leaguer was coming into his own before his eyes and under his direction. And yet he would soon be shipping him back to the minors, probably for keeps.

That really happened sometimes. All platitudes to the contrary, true value was not always fully recognized. If Walker wound up spending his whole baseball life in the minor leagues, he would not be the first true major-leaguer who had done it. Jug Slavin scowled. A baseball manager, in the course of a career, sometimes has to make decisions which do not make him feel proud of himself.

He thought of Devlin's power and agility and color, his favor with the crowd and the front office. Walker had none of these things. What Walker had was a quiet thing never noticed by the crowd, often not noticed by the team, but always felt by them. Slavin felt it. There clung to his mind the memory of the month of September and what a nightmare it always was when you were right in there contending for the pennant, which the Sox would be this year. The last stretch was heartbreaking when you didn't have the pitching. When the September heat came on, you didn't have a thing if you didn't have that pitching. It was the month when, if the starters didn't last, a manager went crazy trying to juggle the staff, watching his good rotation fall apart. But if when that time came, the pitching held up the way it had these past few weeks with Walker in there, nobody could keep this team from a pennant. However, the front office had made a million dollars out of the Sox by keeping it a team of stars. And Walker was no star, while Devlin was.

Slavin got up and started for the field, where the Sox were having early batting practice. It would be his first look at Devlin since the team had left for the West, and from all reports Devlin's recovery had been truly amazing.

Amazing was the word, all right. Jug walked out onto the field and saw Devlin standing in the batting cage, taking pokes at balls served up by old Tweet Tillman, who always liked to keep busy doing something. Tweet was a tireless man, interested in everything, and bound in due time to become a great manager himself. Half of the Sox roster was strung around the cage, watching Devlin. Jug moved over in back of the bunch behind the cage.

Devlin saw Jug and waved at him.

"How is it?" Jug called.

"Great," Devlin called back. "I've got almost the full use of the arm now. Look, I can roll it and bend it." He did both, for proof. "And I'm not just pulling the ball now, Skip. I'm hitting it all over. Watch."

Jug watched. Devlin was lovely to look at, big and tapering, with powerful wrists. He stood there and simply met Tweet Tillman's lobs. He didn't swing hard, but he was meeting the ball perfectly. He rifled a line drive into left field. He shot another into right center. And another into left. Then he swung late but all the way around, and sent a steaming liner which almost carried into the distant bull pen in right field.

"Bet I could hit one out of here today," he boasted exultantly, "no matter who those Clippers pitch."

"Take it easy," Jug told him.

"That's what I've been doing," he yelled. "I'm sick of taking it easy. Me, I want action."

Jug turned away. Devlin wanted action and the chances were he'd get it soon enough. How could you keep a guy like that out of your line-up? Jug shook his head. Walker wasn't the man behind the eight ball; he was worse off than that. He was the man *behind* the man behind the eight ball.

CHAPTER

22

ALTHOUGH DRESSED IN HIS UNIFORM, BUD WAS STILL in the locker room while Jug Slavin was out on the field watching Devlin display his post-operation form. He had gone up; he had reached the mouth of the tunnel that led onto the field and he had seen the exhibition going on. But he had no desire to join in welcoming Devlin back. Devlin had been standing at the plate, swinging freely, playing up to the enthusiastic crowd who watched every move he made. The crowd was made up of Sox players, reporters—and Jug Slavin. Bud had turned around, gone back to the deserted dressing room, and oiled his glove a while to kill time. From the limber look of Devlin he knew that his own time was running out fast. He heard the door open and when he looked up, Devlin walked inside.

Devlin glanced at him with a sneer on his face. He said, "What's the matter? Are you too important these days to get out early with the rest of us? Maybe you think you're a regular now!"

Bud looked at him, wondering why, at the very first moment, Devlin was picking a fight again. Well, he really knew why. Any friction that Devlin could stir up would work to his own advantage. The team couldn't put up with constant friction; if it continued, one of them would have to go. And of course it wouldn't be Devlin. He was a bright boy. He knew that.

Bud said, "The layoff didn't change you any. You still use your mouth too much."

"It didn't change me a bit," Devlin said, "because I still don't care deeply for you, Walker."

"Well, don't think that isn't mutual."

"You were always a busher and you still are. Now that I'm back, you'll find it out."

"You can knock off that busher talk. What makes you keep picking arguments with me, Devlin? Are you afraid of me? Is that it?"

"Afraid of *you?* Afraid of a busher?"

"I told you once to knock that off."

"And if I don't?"

Bud stood up. "This room doesn't look very big. Not big enough for both of us, I guess."

"It won't have to be that big much longer."

Bud started toward the door. Devlin stood in front of it and he didn't budge. Bud said, "Actually, you're not too bright. You keep needling me, which is foolish, because I don't needle easily."

Now he had reached Devlin, who still blocked

the path between the benches to the door. Bud had a choice to make: he could walk around Devlin, stepping over one of the benches, or he could shove Devlin out of his way. Devlin waited and watched as he advanced. The eyes of both men were locked in a look of mutual hostility and contempt. The moment had come now that they had been building up to since they met in Florida. They were both ready and eager to trade swings.

But the doorway behind them was suddenly filled by the bulky form of Jug Slavin. With one quick look he saw everything that was going on and everything that was likely to go on. It was not hard to see.

"Break this stuff up," Jug said.

Devlin turned and stepped to one side, out of Jug's way. Bud didn't move.

"If you two want to fight, then fight. But not here in the clubhouse, where the reporters can make a nice juicy story out of it. Somewhere else."

He walked past them as though he had no further interest in the matter. Then he stopped and turned around. "The next time there's any of this stuff between you, one of you goes. I can't hope to win a pennant with a couple of clubhouse welterweights on my hands. Pretty soon you'll have the whole team picking fights. Now I've warned you both and this is the final warning."

Bud walked out of the door, down the tunnel,

and up to the field. The rage he felt inside himself hadn't started to subside as he picked a bat from the rack and headed toward the cage.

He stepped inside the batting cage and faced young Herb Ward, who was throwing them in. This was Herb's second year up and he still shaved only twice a week. He had been a relief man so far, but he would be a fullfledged starter next year, or maybe before this season ended. Bud wished he had a little more of Herb's way of looking at baseball. Big odds didn't bother Herb.

He was a rugged, confident young man. His manner, his actions, the way he held his head and walked in when flagged from the bull pen—all reflected his complete confidence in himself. He showed the same poise in defeat that he showed in victory. He had the same absorbed concentration lobbing in these batting-practice pitches that he had when he came into a game late, with the bases full and the outcome hanging on each baseball that he threw.

On the mound he was a smooth sweep of power, with his fine, easy windup and perfect follow-through. He always finished each pitch, even in practice, ready to field anything hit his way; they called him a fifth infielder. When pitching a regular game, he used a three-quarter overhand motion. He usually broke his curve ball low and kept his snapping fast one below the waist.

He was never afraid to throw the first one down the middle and dare the sluggers to slug it—a simple thing, but a lot of pitchers never worked up the nerve to do it. "Sure," he explained. "Sometimes they hit it. And hard. But usually I've got enough hop on my fast one so they don't reach the bleachers with it. And I've got Willard, Valenti, and Fiske out there, haven't I? They get paid real good dough. I give 'em a chance to earn it. I'm not out after the strike-out record."

Bud remembered another thing he had said. "If the guy at the plate lets the first one go by—and with me, it's usually a strike—I don't fool around with the next one. I pour it through there, chop-chop, and then the poor dope has to swing in self-defense or leave the bat on his shoulder for strike two. Only difference I see between the big leagues and the minors, anyway, is that up here you can't wonder if you're better than the other fellow. You've got to know you are."

That was a philosophy Bud realized he didn't have, and he needed it. It was hard to acquire such a point of view when you had spent your whole career in the shadow of brilliant performers like Shore and Devlin. But Bud knew he would have to emerge from that shadow somehow, or never be a big-leaguer.

Herb threw the first pitch down the middle and Bud promptly clubbed it into left field.

"Hey, slugger!" Herb yelled enthusiastically. "You got rhythm, like it says in the song."

"If I could bat against your hard one in the games," Bud called back, "I'd be hitting .400."

"Yeah? Well, hit this."

He broke off a jug-handle curve and Bud caught only a small piece of it. The ball skidded weakly down toward third, where the tireless Tweet Tillman grabbed it and heaved toward second base. It went wild, out to the deepest recesses of right field.

Tweet cupped his glove and yelled cheerfully at Herb, "That was my double play around the horn, Herbie boy. That's another jam I pulled you out of."

"Yeah," Herb said. "As a third baseman you're the greatest thing since the banana split."

"Pitch, Herbie boy," Tweet said. "We're all behind you, kid. Nothing to worry about."

Herb pitched and Bud swung. He drove the ball deep to right center. And suddenly he was feeling good again, lifted out of the moody depression that Devlin had managed to create. Jug was right, of course: a team shot full of ill feeling was not a winning team. The spirit that Herb and Tweet displayed was the kind you had to catch and keep. Bud had caught it right now and he didn't want to lose it. Today was going to be a rough day and a real test.

CHAPTER

23

BEFORE GAME TIME BUD KNEW HE FACED AN EVEN
more severe test than he had anticipated—and not
because of Devlin. Because of the crowd. Never
before had he felt the full impact of a crowd's hostility. It was like a cannon fired directly at him.

In the first place, it was a capacity crowd. There
wasn't a vacant gap for a single additional fan to sit
down anywhere in the whole stadium, unless he
wanted to straddle one of the steel girders that
propped up the second deck of the grandstand.
Even the aisles were jammed with people hunched
up knee to knee, and the small section of bleachers
in dead center field, usually kept clear because it
was directly in line with the batter's vision, was now
a solid mass of humanity.

That wasn't all. President O'Neill was there.
O'Neill seldom could tear himself away from his
battery of telephones long enough to watch his ex-
pensive talent in action. But he had today. He sat

in his royal box above the second deck, close to the radio and television booths.

Bud thought, I'd better be good today. I'd better not make any mistakes or this mob will tear me apart.

What put the last ounce of pressure on him was the fact that most of this pennant-hungry crowd had seen Devlin performing as flashily as ever in practice. As far as they could tell, their fair-haired boy, their pennant insurance, looked ready for the wars again. The newspapers had implied as much, hadn't they? As a result, when the public-address system announced the starting line-up, with Walker on second, the surging brutality of the crowd's reaction hit him physically. It hit him in the pit of the stomach, like a wave of gas escaping from a leaky pipe. He had expected the booing. But the fierceness of it almost knocked him over.

When the Sox sprang from the dugout, Bud didn't quite spring. He stepped out cautiously, warily, as if into the face of gunfire. As though to vindicate his instinctive hesitation, there burst from the hostile mass of blue and white shirts a terrifying roar made up of two parts anger and one part resentment. At first it was blurred and indistinct, because it was not synchronized. Then, gradually, it pulled itself together, until it rocked out clearly and sharply, turning into a rhythmic chant, jungle-like in its monotony and intensity.

"We want Devlin! We want Devlin! We want
Devlin! We want Devlin! We want. . . ."

Trotting along to position beside Bates, Bud
heard Bates say something to him. He couldn't
catch it over the crowd's jungle chant, but he knew
that Bates was trying to say something encouraging,
something to bolster his spirit in the face of the
crowd's unjust rejection. He could only nod and
grunt the deep appreciation that he felt toward
Bates for his gesture of friendship at this critical
moment.

He scooped up the grounder that Blake threw to
him. He threw it back to Blake. Six straight we've
won, he thought, and now we're after our seventh.
This should be a happy crowd. But six straight
didn't suit them. Why not? All they felt was that
this was a team which had won a pennant and a
World Series last year. Now they were in second
place playing the Clippers, who were in first place.
And the Clippers had a clean record against them
so far of three won and none lost.

Yank Yoland was pitching for the Sox today.
Yank was the type of pitcher who was tough but
often had a bad first inning. If he got through the
first, he almost always went nine. But you had to
worry about his first inning. It meant that right at
the start the heavy pressure was on the Sox. They
all knew. They all hoped.

The Clipper lead-off man was Palazzo, their

midget shortstop. Palazzo was hard to pitch to, which was why he led off. He was extremely short and he crouched and he had twenty-twenty vision —a sound combination for a lead-off man.

Yank missed the strike zone with his first four pitches. Palazzo trotted happily down to first, like a kid with his first jackknife. The stands rumbled. The Sox knew they were in for one of Yank's usual bad first innings. And when Yank had a bad first inning, the rest of the team might just as well have been sitting on a volcano.

Woodlund, the Clippers' left fielder, stepped in, and the Sox infield crept closer to the plate. They were prepared for a bunt, of course, but they were not sure of it. Woodlund was a slash hitter, and the Clippers had never been noted for doing what was expected of them.

Woodlund took a ball. Then a strike. It was the first strike Yank had managed to throw, and the crowd gave it a big, faintly derisive cheer.

Yank missed the corner again. He promptly followed with the good one, too good, the one that Woodlund had been longing for. Woodlund did not lay it down; he slashed away and the ball shot into center field like a dog that had sighted a rabbit.

Palazzo had been off with the pitch. He reached third standing up while Madigan stood there, going through the faking motion of a man about to receive an outfield throw. Madigan liked to make runners

slide needlessly, just to watch them wear out their
pants.

Men on first and third now. Nobody out. Yoland's discouraging first-inning pattern was taking
shape. But it was not yet quite complete.

Bower, the third Clipper hitter, seemed to be
working on the theory that the fine edge of Yank's
control had not yet been achieved, and the theory
paid off. Yank threw him five pitches. They were
all so close to the strike zone that from the stands
you could have flipped a coin to decide. But the
umpire was not in the stands; he stood directly behind the plate, and he did not need a coin. He
called one of them a strike and four of them balls.
Bower ambled down to first, loading the bags with
nobody out. A resentful groan rose from the crowd
and, as it did, the pitchers in the Sox bull pen rose
too.

Gibbs pushed his mask back over his head and
strode out, mitt on hip, to talk to Yank. Madigan,
who always had to be in on eveything, strolled over.
They looked as grave as a directors' meeting. When
they finally broke up, Madigan reluctantly returned
to third, still muttering.

Big De Lucca, the Clipper clean-up man, waited
at the plate like a gangster with a gun at his victim's
head. He always looked menacing anyway, but
especially with the bases full. De Lucca was having a very bad year so far, for him—a measly .336.

De Lucca figured, apparently, that Yank would take good care not to get behind the batter in this dangerous spot. He seemed to think that Yank would come in with the first pitch, and rightly so. Yank came in with it. De Lucca was consequently waiting to greet it with everything short of a brass band.

De Lucca was a right-handed pull hitter who still didn't know his own strength after seven years in the majors. He swung from a flat-footed stance with the impact of a pile driver and sent Yank's overeager strike screaming down the third-base foul line. It was authoritatively aimed for the distant left-field bleacher wall, apparently good for two bases and maybe three, which would mean two runs and maybe three.

But the incredible Madigan could make a magician look slow and awkward. Somehow he was there, with a backhand twist of his glove. The ball was pretty deep at the point where he got it, but he got it. It was too deep for a play at the plate, because the runner from third had made an instantaneous start. Madigan turned and shot the ball to second.

Bud had never expected Madigan to come up with the ball, but he was there waiting for Madigan's throw. A double play around the horn is a long, long haul in any case. But this particular one had a minimum number of seconds to complete the circuit because of the distance behind third at which the ball had been snared. Madigan's hasty throw was a little high. But Bud swooped it in. He touched the bag as he did, shot into the air as the runner hit him, and then went down in a heap on top of him, but not before he got the ball off to Blake.

When he disentangled himself from Bower, he saw the first-base umpire's thumb jerked upward. He saw the look of incredulous relief on the face of Yank Yoland. He saw the look of utter disgust on the face of Bower.

Bower got up and batted the dust from his uniform. As he headed toward the Clipper bench, he growled over his shoulder, "What'd you use—a slingshot?"

That did it. The pressure was off. Yank Yoland found that little lost thread of control. He touched the corners on the next hitter. Gibbs smothered a foul pop for the unexpectedly quick third out.

As the team trooped into the dugout, that one-run lead the Clippers had looked like nothing. The debacle had been averted. The applause thundered out but of course it was all for Madigan, who deserved it.

Just the same, Bud thought, Devlin could not have done it. Never.

As if to confirm his opinion, Madigan touched his arm. Madigan said, "You got it off like a pistol, kid. It was a rough one to put the glue on."

Yank Yoland grinned at him too. Yank said, "I always claimed there wasn't any defense against the base on balls. Brother, I take it all back now. That kinda double play is really it."

The wolves would howl at Bud all day, sure. But this team, or some of it, knew he wasn't exactly dragging them down.

CHAPTER

24

THAT FIRST-INNING DOUBLE PLAY WHICH HAD snatched Yank clear of danger seemed to act like a tonic to him. He settled down firmly and it was a very fortunate thing. Because Tim Flagg, the Clipper pitcher, was an old pro who knew how to be just as good as he had to be. He saw by the look of things that this was one of those days when he would have to treat that single run as though it were the last dollar in his bank account. And he proceeded to act as though it were as big a nest egg as he needed.

Except for the first inning, however, Yank matched him zero for zero on the scoreboard. Bud marveled at the sudden and complete way that Yank had got a grip on himself and on his delicate little thread of control. He watched Yank drive the Clipper hitters back from the plate with inside balls, then zip the edge of the outside corner while he still had them loosened up. Yank always said he figured he had just about two dozen hard pitches in his arm per nine innings, and he had to ration those carefully among the special spots where they were needed most.

In the course of a season a fair number of home runs were always hit off Yank, but that did not distress him or anyone else very much, because his won-and-lost record and his earned-run average were always better than respectable. He hadn't been just kidding when he told Bud that he always claimed there was no defense against the base on balls.

"That's why," he had once explained, "I'm always trying to make a man hit a ball, no matter where he hits it. I'd rather risk a homer than a base on balls, for a fact. The way the ball is souped up today, a guy who doesn't throw any faster than I do doesn't dare make more than one mistake. A pitcher who can power the ball on every pitch can get away with two or three mistakes. But me, I can't give a thing away. And with the supercharged ball we use now, I figure the home run alone isn't the real sin. The real sin is the home run following the base on balls."

Knowing this pitching philosophy of Yank's, Bud found it doubly interesting to watch him weave his way through the big Clipper guns, inning after inning. If you could call pitching an art, then Yank was one of the real artists.

He was striking no Clippers out, but after that first inning he was walking none, either. They were banging many long outfield balls off his delivery, some of them dangerously close to the bleacher walls, yet none of them had quite enough carry to drop into the seats. They came to rest harmlessly and accomplished nothing more than keeping Willard, Valenti, and Fiske busy. The singles and doubles that he gave up were judiciously scattered. Yank's really hard pitch could only be observed when it was really needed for the third strike with a runner in scoring position.

If the Sox could have punctured Flagg's self-possession at all, the game would have been as easy to take as a breeze. But they couldn't make a dent on Flagg. It was the fourth inning before the first safe blow was struck by a Blue Sox batsman, and that was just a blooper single to right by Fiske.

The inning before that, Bud had made a real bid for a Texas leaguer to center, but big De Lucca had glided in like a gull and snatched it off his shoe tops. For this effort the crowd had given Bud a well-sustained hoot as he trotted in to the dugout, even though he was the eighth man to face Flagg and the eighth man to fail. He saw even this early that in the eyes of this crowd he simply could do nothing right.

The game was going along like the hands on a clock, with time working for Flagg and running out on Yank. Then, in the bottom of the eighth, Bud led off. The Sox were six outs away now from their fourth straight defeat at the hands of the Clippers, six outs away from the end of their six-game winning streak.

Bud hadn't made a hit yet, but neither had most of the other Sox; they had a team total of only four. A base hit off Flagg today was a rare item. Flagg promptly put Bud in a one-and-two hole and then broke a curve across. Bud had to swing in self-defense or go down looking. He punched at it, met it weakly, and sent it skidding down to short, an easy-looking chance. The crowd groaned. It was the hopeless kind of thing that many batters give up on as they go down to first. But Bud didn't give up.

He raced down the line, legs pumping with every ounce of drive he could give them, and the hustle paid off. The easy throw came in low and when the first baseman scooped at it, the ball bounced off his glove and Bud was safe on the error.

Flagg looked annoyed. He glared at Yank Yoland, now up at bat, as though Yank were the single man at the root of all the world's troubles. Yank got set to bunt, but Flagg crossed him up and the bunt did not tuck itself down on the turf. It popped. Flagg handled it the way a mackerel handles a minnow. It was a quick snatch and he whirled and threw to first almost in the same motion. But Bud, who had checked his start for second, turned, dove headfirst at the bag, and made it.

At least, the umpire thought so, though nine other people loudly expressed an opposite opinion—and all nine wore uniforms with Clipper lettering across the chest. But no team ever altered that kind of a decision, and the Clippers grumbled their way back to their positions without having broken any precedents in the matter.

Madigan stepped up and Tweet Tillman, coaching at third, flashed the hit-and-run sign. Bud lit out for second on the first pitch and, as the Clipper second baseman promptly darted to his right to cover the bag, Madigan punched a hard ground ball exactly into the hole thus created. That sent Bud into third without strain, and the crowd woke up.

But in the next moment they were groaning again. Fiske, also going for the first pitch, bounced a ground ball down to big Maze, the Clipper first baseman. Bud had been started on his way by Tillman, with the swing. Now Maze came up with a play that was very alert. He shot the ball across the infield to Jensen, the Clipper third baseman, and there was Bud, trapped in the string play, the fall guy in a routine and inevitable rundown between third and home. It was a trap without an escape, but though he looked as futile as a man on a treadmill, he darted back and forth, back and forth, as long as he could elude the tag, in order to give Madigan time to reach third and Fiske time to reach second. That was his only mission—or the only one usual in such a situation.

But Bud had other ideas. With Jensen, Flagg, and Burrow, the Clipper catcher, closing in on him, there seemed no doubt that he was now practically a dead duck. But as he reversed his field for about the tenth time—and at the precise moment when Jensen caught a quick return from Burrow—Bud plunged smack into Burrow. Burrow stood in his path, on the base line. But Burrow, as Bud saw when he smacked him, did not have the ball.

When Bud and Burrow crashed, Jensen jumped from behind and clamped the tag on Bud. But even before he saw Jug Slavin bound out of the dugout and start to shout a single word at the umpire, Bud shouted that one word himself: *"Obstruction!"*

Burrow, Jensen, and Flagg all heard the word, and their faces froze in horror as the umpire nodded and waved Bud on to the plate. Bud crossed it and turned to watch what was happening, his face one great big grin. The Clipper dugout was emptying, and every face was irate. Burrow, Jensen, and Flagg surrounded the umpire, hands on hips, faces red with anger, and fear growing in their eyes.

The umpire's voice bellowed clearly from the midst of them. "The run scores and that's according to the rule book. Obstruction by Burrow on the base path without possession of the ball. You can look it up."

Shanty Millikin, the granite-faced Clipper manager, screamed, "Obstruction my eye! He rammed him! Walker rammed him when he knew Burrow didn't have the ball. It was a trick, I tell you, a trick!"

"According to the official rules . . ." the umpire droned.

"You letting that wise cookie get away with this?"

"Play ball!" the umpire bellowed.

At the dugout step Jug Slavin regarded Bud with wonder in his eyes. "You ever been mixed up in the—ummm—obstruction play before, Walker?" he said.

"A couple of times," Bud said with a grin. "These catchers always like to hog the base line."

"It was an accident, of course," Jug said, the wonder still in his eyes, "and a mighty opportune one for us. Yes indeed, indeed."

That was an understatement, as things turned out, because Flagg, fired to dizzy heights by his fury, struck out both Valenti and Blake. That meant that if it had not been for the obstruction play on the rundown, the Sox would not have gone out for the start of the ninth with a tie score to keep them alive.

The ninth was scoreless. So was the tenth, and the eleventh. In the top of the twelfth, however, Yank showed signs of being close to the end of his vast reservoir of craft and energy. After one out, two straight singles put him in a bad jam. And the second hit was followed by a hard smash aimed at the hole between short and third.

Bates went to his right with the eager greed of a spider and gobbled it up. He flipped to Bud, who made the pivot and got the snap throw off to Blake. That pulled Yank through, but he looked done in as he shambled from the mound. Out in the bull pen, Herb Ward was warming up fast.

Gibbs, the first Sox hitter in the last of the twelfth, probed Flagg's condition and found it to be sinking too. He doubled wickedly to left center. That brought Bud up, thinking that finally he had a chance to play the hero's role.

He should have known better.

True, one little single would break up the ball game, and he was due for a hit. But Slavin had other strategy in mind. It was evident that a pinch hitter would replace Yank. That, no doubt, was why Bud got the bunt signal from Tillman.

So he was still the straight man. His job was to get Gibbs to third and set up the hero's role for somebody else. Gibbs would not need a hit to bring him in from third; a long fly or a deep grounder would do it.

Bud laid one down on the third pitch, a neat one that he narrowly missed beating out. That put Gibbs on third and gave somebody else the hero's role. Bud knew, when he made the turn at first and heard the shriek of delight from the stands, who had been selected for it. But just to confirm his suspicion, he took a quick look.

Sure enough, standing in the on-deck circle and swinging three bats with picturesque abandon was Devlin. Destiny's tot, Bud thought. That's what he is.

The crowd was up on its feet now. Flagg looked tired. Burrow, Jensen, and Maze walked over to confer. The only apparent result was that Burrow, Jensen, and Maze began to look tired too. They ought to walk him, Bud thought, and set up the double play. But with Devlin's luck anything could be expected to happen.

Devlin's luck held. The Clippers didn't walk him. They gambled. Bud could see why, at that. They figured he had been out so long that his eye and his timing might be off. And Madigan, who followed, would probably not hit a double-play ball, because he was very swift going down the line and he was also a master of the squeeze bunt. On a one-out situation, Madigan would get that run in.

So they pitched to Devlin. A strike. A ball. A second ball. Then another strike, and Devlin swung.

The ball sailed out, floating like a dirigible. It had not really been well struck, but it had a wind behind it. Woodlund's back was by no means at the wall as the ball dropped into his glove for an easy out, but Gibbs, for a catcher, was a fast man. Woodlund gunned the throw in but Palazzo cut it off, because it clearly wasn't any contest. So there was the ball game.

As Bud headed toward the gate, he glanced back and saw that the fans who had spilled over the grandstand railing were all but mobbing Devlin. Bud thought of how he had twice been in the middle of tough double plays that had saved the game; and how it never even would have gone into extra innings if he hadn't maneuvered the obstruction play; and how he had been the stooge to set up the hero's role for Devlin. And what was the final result of all this? Devlin was walking off the field with all the glory securely tucked in his hip pocket.

He's just the kind of a guy, Bud thought, who could fall into a haystack and come up with a corner on the needle market.

CHAPTER

25

WELL ANYWAY, BUD THOUGHT THE NEXT DAY, WHO wants glory? Let them look at the record—seven straight now, and the Clipper jinx broken. All this done with Walker at second. No, Walker's not hitting .300. Matter of fact, he's only hitting .247. But never mind the personal records. Look at the team records.

By any standards Bud should have felt secure in his job. He had earned the right, it would seem, to feel that he had made good, even on this team of stars. And yet, as he headed toward the stadium for the second game of this Clipper series, he had a hunch he would watch this one from the bench.

The accounts in the morning paper had been glowing—about Devlin and what the team would do, now that he was ready. They admitted that Walker had been in the ball game. But Devlin had won it. Devlin was the hero.

Let's not be bitter, Bud told himself. After all, I've got my health. That's more than O'Neill can

say. He's not eating crackers and milk because he
prefers that as a lunch.

Among the fans and the writers there was a rising
sense of overconfidence in the Sox, and it was all
based on the theory that the Sox had done as well
as they had in spite of Devlin's absence. Jug Slavin
must have felt that this was not so. Bud had read
Ed Daly's column that morning, an interview with
Jug, and Jug had obviously been trying to indicate
a state of affairs nearer the truth.

"After that great victory we earned in the play-off
game last fall, followed by our victory over the
Robins in the World Series, everybody started to
pick us as a sure thing to win again this year. They
were talking through their hats. That was a lot of
wishful thinking.

"In the first place, winning the second consec-
utive pennant is always tough. How many teams
ever do repeat without skipping a year or two or
many more in between? You can count them on
your thumbs, not fingers.

"This is due partly to the way the opposition feels
about you and partly to the way you feel about
yourself. I mean, it's easy for a ball club to get too
satisfied, too contented, after they have won the
Series. You can get overconfident and uncon-
sciously relax. One of the biggest jobs a manager
ever has to face is that of getting a championship
club keyed up again when it has let down.

"To make that even tougher, when you've won one year, the rest of the league really guns for you the next. Everybody wants to beat the favorite. They save their best pitchers for you. If one of their regulars has been out for a few days, you can count on him returning to the line-up the day you come to town. Repeating is tough. It takes a real good, solid club to turn the trick, believe me.

"And there's another vital point, too. A managerial job essential to success is the fitting of new pieces into the worn-out parts of a championship outfit. You can have all the talent in the world on tap, but you've got to pick the right stuff, the special stuff that fits into the whole cloth. You don't make such decisions merely by looking at a man's batting average or the width of his shoulders.

"Few winning clubs can repeat without one or two changes, and picking kids to replace aging veterans is not always as simple as it looks. We could all see before we went to spring training this year that we could not possibly present ourselves as a strong contender until we had found a real big-league catcher to take Tweet Tillman's place, and a real big-league second baseman to take Shore's place. Well, last year's play-off game and the Series that followed proved beyond a doubt that we had found our catcher in Pete Gibbs, the guy who had never before been able to shake off the belief that he was strictly a catcher from Double-A.

"Second base was a horse of another color. It was a problem yet to be settled. As it's turned out,

we've got two good second basemen, but of course
there's only room for one. The question from the
start was, which one fitted better into the scheme
of things, the slightly broken pattern of this team.
It's not entirely in the batting averages. But the
point is, anyone who thinks the Sox are a cinch for
the second championship in a row is kidding himself. As the guy responsible for bringing this semi-
miracle to pass, I'm against all such irresponsible
talk, and you can quote me."

That was not the most discouraging piece in the
world, Bud thought. Slavin had not come out full
blast with any decisive Devlin-is-the-man talk.
Studying it carefully, Bud could see the lingering
doubt in Jug's mind about second base. Yet he
knew, of course, that Jug's hands were tied. The
crowd and the front office combined to make a force
too strong for a mere manager to overcome. And
if a manager couldn't overcome it, who could?

He told himself, as he walked into the locker
room at the stadium prepared for the worst, that he
might as well face the fact that baseball was big
business and that Devlin represented a big profit
to the club in terms of bonus investment and drawing power at the home gate. Bud couldn't do much
more than he had done except hit better, as he knew
he could with a sense of security behind him. But
all he had done wasn't enough and the end was

nearly in sight. He felt that—in his head, in his heart, and even in his bones.

He was not at all surprised, therefore, when the bat boy came up to him as he got into his uniform. He said, "Front and center, Slug. The Skip wants to see you."

"So here's where I get the word," Bud said. "O. K."

He finished dressing and went to Jug's office, where he found him alone, chewing on the stump of a cigar, his face looking as frazzled as the cigar. He seemed by no means as happy as a manager with a seven-game winning streak under his belt should be.

Jug said, "Walker, I had a long talk with O'Neill this morning and I have to report that the situation is nearing the hopeless stage for you. It gives me no pleasure to tell you this, because personally—as I told him—I like the kind of ball you've been playing for me."

"Thanks."

"He wanted me to start Devlin at second this afternoon, but I was able to put my foot down on that. He knows as well as I do that a manager never breaks up a winning combination. It's one of the few baseball superstitions that make sense. I pointed out to him that we've won seven straight now with you at second and that the pitching has been all but foolproof."

"Did—did he have any comment on that?"

"Yes. He said it was a seasonal thing. It had simply settled down through force of habit."

"But I still play today's game."

"Today's and every day's—until we lose one."

"Then I'm all set," Bud said. "All I have to do is see to it that we don't lose one between now and October and I'm in."

"It's just about that hopeless. No manager can buck a front office like this one. On this club, the front office rules with an iron hand. I don't know any force, managerial or otherwise, that can over-rule it."

"It's a funny situation for a guy to be in. Mine, I mean."

"I never heard of one quite like it, to be honest. Here we're going like a house afire with you in and the minute we drop a single game and break that streak, you're out."

"Triple-A then?"

"Not quite. I did get this out of him. I made him promise to let me keep you on the bench for a while anyway. He said I could keep you—but only if you didn't cause any further dissension."

"In other words, if Devlin picks a fight with me I can either take it lying down or I can pack my bag and head for Triple-A."

"You're on a spot, kid, and I know it. I wish there were some way I could buck this front office. But there isn't. As far as I know, nothing short of a miracle can dislodge their golden bonus boy."

"I'm no great believer in miracles."

"Neither am I. But—don't stop hustling, kid."

"I won't," Bud told him. "I wouldn't know how."

"I can almost believe that," Jug said.

CHAPTER

26

BUD HAD NOT BEEN FOOLING WHEN HE TOLD JUG HE wouldn't know how to stop hustling. He had spoken in all honesty. He had never played ball any other way and it was too late to change now. That was a good thing, because if it had not been an ingrained habit, he would surely have found it hard to do his best today.

Comparatively speaking, yesterday had been a honeymoon, but that didn't shock him; it didn't even surprise him. He had known it would be that way when he walked out on the field and faced another capacity crowd, their anger justified today by the newspapers' glowing accounts of their boy, Devlin. Now that Devlin had returned and played the hero's role, they had thought nothing could keep him out of the line-up. They had reckoned without one of the most deeply rooted of all baseball superstitions.

Now, for the first time, Bud accepted as inescapable the fact that today, and every day from now on,

might be the last one for him. Nothing was going
to change that fact. Nothing could. Reluctantly,
gently, but definitely, Jug Slavin had just finished
making that crystal clear.

Bud had not realized until this moment when all
real hope was cut out from under him just how
much of a blow it would be to him to leave this
team. They were not a team of strangers any more.
They were a bunch of guys he had lived with,
fought the good fight with, traded jokes with, day
in and day out. That made a difference. At first it
had been just the fear of leaving behind a chance
for recognition and the big money. Now it was a
matter of leaving his friends behind. Because they
had become friends, warm ones. He liked them and
they liked him. A close feeling had come out of all
that shared sweat and pressure.

Even if Jug had not given him the final sentence,
Bud would have known that his number was really
up. It was not just that the crowd's hostility was
much sharper and much louder. It was the actual
rage they projected when they found him still at
second base and their hero back on the bench.
Their surging resentment was a brutal thing to hear
—especially if your name was Walker.

But even if your name wasn't Walker, if you were
just somebody who wore blue stockings and a white
uniform with blue stripes, you felt the force of it.
Because today the crowd spread their abuse around

with a free hand. They gave Jug Slavin a dose of it
every time he stuck his head out of the dugout.
They gave the other eight men in the line-up a dose
of it every time any one of them made a move that
was less than perfect. The fans' feeling toward their
team was something thick enough to cut.

It represented pure fan mutiny of an almost incredible sort: mutiny against a team that was
steadily ticking off victories. Still, it did not seem
to demoralize the team any more than it demoral-
ized Bud. And he made two singles and got a base
on balls in five trips to the plate. He was flawless in
the field, even occasionally brilliant. But the crowd
crowned him with derision.

It was a grim, tight-lipped Sox team that faced
it down and trounced the cocky, league-leading
Clippers for the second day in succession, running
their own winning streak up to eight. All afternoon
the crowd remained silent when the Sox gave them
reason to cheer. All afternoon they became noisily
articulate when the Clippers gave them a chance
to jeer the home team.

By the time the papers came out the next morning, Bud's unique position in the starting line-up
was no longer a secret. The writers told the world
that he was in to stay, come what might, until the
Sox winning streak ended. And then he was
through. So that much was settled. At least the
situation wasn't hazy any more. The fans knew

where they stood and where Walker stood. Ed Daly wrote:

> This Sox team is probably the first winning team in the stadium's history which grows more unpopular with the crowd every time it wraps up another ball game. Ridiculous as it may sound, the only way the Sox are going to get their fans rooting for them again is to lose a ball game so the crowd can have what they want—Devlin at second. Bud Walker, meanwhile, is bearing the brunt of the deadliest abuse campaign I've ever seen pulled off in the big leagues, but don't think the rest of the team is having the whip spared. Walker can't hope to win in the end, as he and the team must know, but he has certainly turned into an amazing *cause célèbre* in this incredible feud between a ball club and its fans. The situation is one for the books, but it can't last long. In fact, I'd be willing to bet that it ends today.

Bud would not have blamed the rest of the team for resenting his presence, for without him they would have had none of this trouble. But there was no resentment in them: there was a hard core of solidarity, more of a one than he had ever felt on the team before. On the field they acted more like fighting-mad sand-lot kids than high-priced pros, but their anger was directed toward the fans, not toward Bud. They acted almost protective toward him. When he made a good play or a timely hit, someone was always quick to show him by word or gesture that they were proud of him. When catcalls and boos were showered upon him, they were equally quick to speak to him, to say something that made him feel not entirely alone.

During the second Clipper game, for instance, he struck out after making two straight singles, and when he went out to his position in the next inning the crowd let him have a tremendous volley of jeers. Bates, trotting out shoulder to shoulder with him, said, "Those dopes! They still think they can make you crack."

"How could they?" Bud said. "What can they yell that they haven't yelled before?"

During the third and last game of the Clipper series, the crowd started cheering for the Clippers from the first inning on. The boos grew louder every time the Sox came up to bat and failed to score. And this game, finally, looked like the end. The Sox hitters could not do a thing. They went into the last of the ninth, trailing 4 to 1.

The mob started to mill happily toward the exit ramps and as they went, they chanted, "Tomorrow Devlin! Tomorrow Devlin!"

Fiske opened the inning by grounding out to first. The crowd roared triumphantly. Valenti momentarily dismayed them when he crashed a long drive to the extreme left-field corner in a bid for extra bases. But Woodlund, in left, leaped high and pulled it down, and the crowd grew hoarse with exultation as Valenti trotted dejectedly back to the dugout.

Two out, nobody on. Still 4 to 1.

Beef Trust Blake stepped in and the crowd screamed derision—the first taste of it he had ever had from them. *"Three outs, Blake! Three outs! Here it is!"*

Blake twisted his size seventeen neck and took a quick glare at them. Then, very deliberately, he spat at the ground. And for answer he swung on the first pitch and really creamed it. It was a rising line drive that fairly sizzled with speed. It would have landed cleanly in the remote center-field bleachers if it had been just one foot higher. Instead, it caromed crazily off the guard rail with big De Lucca frantically chasing it. It was so deep and so elusive that even the lumbering Blake was waved along from third by Tillman in the coaching box. Blake slid, something he seldom did and did not need to do now. He was in with the first inside-the-park homer he had ever hit in his life. The score was 4 to 2 and the Sox were still alive. The crowd was silent. The Sox bench was riotously noisy.

Willard stepped in now. He blasted the two-and-nothing pitch into left field for a single, and the crowd stopped dead in its antlike progress toward the exits.

Bates came up. He worked the count to three-and-two and then belted a double into right center which scored the fleet Willard from first. Now, all of a sudden, it was 4 to 3, with the tying run in scoring position.

Gibbs followed, and Bud stood in the on-deck circle, thinking that if they walked Gibbs to get at him, the ball game would be right in his lap. But the Clipper pitcher had no intention of deliberately putting Gibbs on base with the tie-breaking run. He pitched to Gibbs. He only pitched two balls. The first one was wide. The second one wasn't, and Gibbs swung from the heels.

It was a power pitch and Gibbs answered it with more power. The ball took off on a rising line, just as Blake's had, and it described almost the same arc except that it had about three more feet of height. It did not carom off the guard railing in center field. It carried over it and sent the fans scattering like hornets from a burning nest.

Gibbs was trotting around the bases in a methodical, unhurried fashion. The stands were completely silent. The Sox bench had emptied and a line had formed to greet Gibbs as he crossed the plate with the run that won the ball game, 5 to 4. Bud tossed away the three bats he had been swinging and got in line to greet Gibbs.

That made it a sweep of the Clipper series. That was the ninth straight win for the Sox and put them in a tie with the Clippers for first place. That was the run which meant that Walker would still be playing second base tomorrow.

When he pumped Gibbs' hand, Bud said, "You'll never top that blow, Pete. Never."

"Tomorrow I will," Pete said. "I took aim at a guy in a blue shirt in the fifth row out there. I missed him, but I'll get him tomorrow. Just wait."

CHAPTER

27

THIS BITTER FEUD BETWEEN FANS AND TEAM COULD only be disastrous in terms of winning a pennant, but for the moment it was the greatest thing the stadium box office had ever known. Anger seemed to bring the crowd back in numbers, day after day, in a way that loyalty had never done.

Even though it was the lowly Grays who moved in next, the stadium was a sellout. This amazed the front office boys, who were well aware that the Grays were anything but a stellar attraction. But the fans knew that something was bound to give any moment now. This feud couldn't go on. This winning streak couldn't go on. There was too much pressure all around. Something or somebody had to snap. And nobody wanted to miss the kill.

It came.

Bud felt the pressure during practice. He saw it in the faces of the team, as they got ready to try for ten straight. He saw it in the tight, set expressions of their mouths; the tense way they stood

when they should have been in repose; the narrowed eyes as they looked at each other and especially as they looked at the stands. They were a
truly great team, he thought, with their fine spirit
and the sterling integrity that made them so loyal
to himself, the man who was not really one of them,
but an accident that had happened to them. And
they refused to let him down, because they knew it
was not his fault that the fans had no use for him.
Still, they were human. They had to crack pretty
soon. They had to blow a ball game as all teams,
good or bad, have to sometimes.

Lasky, known as Old Dependable, was pitching
today. But he faced a rough time, because the
Grays had lost six out of their last seven. They were
in the cellar and they were tired of it. They were
angry and frustrated and in a mood to lash out at
anybody, but especially at the league leaders, whose
defeat could give them a particularly soothing balm.
Lasky would need both heart and head to hold
them in line today.

They filled the bases on him in the first inning,
but a Bates-to-Walker-to-Blake double play pulled
him out of that mess as the crowd groaned openly
in dismay.

They were quiet in the second but then came the
third, when a lead-off single and a quick double
put two men in scoring position with nobody out.
Lasky, superbly fearless, came out of it with only

one run marked against him. And just to show him that he wasn't fighting alone, the Sox came right back and matched it for him in their half. Madigan ran himself ragged beating out a bunt. Fiske flied out, but Valenti rapped a double and that tied it up.

Lasky was reached for two singles in the fifth, but Madigan stopped a rifle shot down the foul line and nailed the runner at the plate to save a further score. In the sixth, however, the enraged Grays ganged up on Lasky. They pushed a pair of runs across with a walk and two straight doubles.

It was 3 to 1 now.

In the last half of the same inning the Sox spirit asserted itself again. Bud singled. Lasky bunted him to second. Madigan got robbed on a line drive to third and Bud just dove back in time to escape being doubled. Then Fiske shot a bullet into center and Bud, urged on by desperate coaching abandon, roared for the plate. The throw-in had him licked, but he licked the throw-in with a hook slide that eluded the tag. Valenti flied out, but they had one of those runs back. That was all the scoring that took place until the last of the eighth, when they came to bat, still behind 3 to 2.

Valenti lined to left. Blake flied deep to left. But Willard made a monkey out of the Grays' third baseman, who was playing deep, when he dumped a bunt down the line and beat it out for a scratch single.

Bates moved in and hit one into the left-field corner for two bases. Willard, who could sprint with the best of them, raced across the plate with the run that tied up the ball game. Then Gibbs strode up and when he hit a single to center, everyone in the park knew that Bates would never stop at third, though the single was short.

From the Sox bench, Bud thought Bates was in. But the umpire didn't think so. He jerked the fatal right thumb high into the air.

Bates got up, screaming his rage to the heavens. The umpire turned his back. Jug roared out of the dugout and joined Bates in his outcry. The crowd booed them; for once they were with the umpire.

The Grays trooped in from the field, looking annoyed at the delay which Bates and Jug were causing. Still, Bates and Jug stood chin to chin with the umpire, neither of them at a loss for words.

The umpire warned them. Slavin turned and headed toward the dugout. Those arguments, of course, were always hopeless, but anger made a man hate to quit them. Bates headed toward his position, but his face was red and his steps were slow and grudging. At the mound he turned and shouted something back. Whatever he shouted, it must have been good. Because that did it.

The umpire roared at Bates and jerked his thumb toward the players' gate. Bates started to charge, thought better of it, and shuffled toward the gate.

The crowd jeered him. He was still shouting back at the umpire and at the crowd as he disappeared through the gate.

Jug Slavin was out of the dugout now. Bud was watching Bates disappear through the gate when he heard the roar of exultation that came from the stands. He looked at Jug and then he saw the reason for the roar: behind Jug, glove in hand, was Devlin.

Jug beckoned to Bud. Bud trotted over. Jug's weary face was seamy with troubled lines. He said, in a tired voice, "Get this, the pair of you. I wouldn't throw you together, but Adams has got a Charley horse and nobody else can play short but you, Walker. That's where you play. Devlin plays second. First place and the winning streak are on every pitch. Play ball like grown men." He turned abruptly and walked away.

Bud looked at Devlin and Devlin looked at Bud. "I'm not looking for trouble if you're not, Devlin," Bud said.

Devlin just smiled and walked off toward his position. Bud turned and trotted toward his. Jug was right, of course. First place, too, was on this game. The scoreboard showed that the Clippers had already won their game. First place, the winning streak, and Walker—they all rode on this game now.

Lasky had his ball game tied up for him, but he

looked tired. He proved he was by walking the first man. The second one laid down a bunt that moved the runner up. The third one slapped a pitch into left field for a clean single, but the runner held at third, because the single had not gone deep and Willard had a slingshot arm that was no secret. So there were men on first and third with one out, and Lasky looked like celery that had been left out of the icebox overnight.

Slavin strode out of the dugout, waved at the bull pen, and that was that. Herb Ward, who had been warming up off and on since the seventh, started to make the long trek in—jauntily, cockily, confidently. Lasky stood dejectedly on the mound, awaiting his arrival, while Blake and Madigan walked over to him for a brief conversation that did not appear to be of the intellectual type.

Devlin was standing on the bag, his arms folded. Bud edged over and said, "Look, Devlin. I'm no shortstop."

"Yeah. I surmised that."

"The thing is, this hitter is a lefty and Herb will keep them low for a D. P. ball which, if he hits it, will probably go to you."

"How elementary can you get, Walker?"

"What I'm trying to tell you is this: if you get the D. P. ball, which looks likely, feed it to me shoulder high, on the left side. You got that?"

"I always feed it that way."

"O. K. Just so we got it straight. A D. P. ball is a lifesaver right now."

Devlin turned away. Bud turned away. Devlin called back, "Where did you think I'd feed it— across the ankles?"

Bud wanted to scream at him. He bit his lip and said, "Just so you know where I need to get it."

Herb Ward finished his warm-up pitches. The Sox got set in position. Herb glanced around, looking cool and unruffled, as he always did. He took the stretch and threw.

The first one, at the knees, missed the corner. So did the second. The third one was at the knees, but in. The batter swung.

The ball was clipped hard, on the ground, right at Devlin. He was in perfect position. It was a double-play ball. It was labeled end of the inning. He gobbled it up. He turned and snapped. Bud was there, waiting. But the throw wasn't shoulder-high. It wasn't to his left. Nobody, with all that time at his command, could have made a throw so wrong without meaning to make it wrong.

Bud got it on the right, at his knees. He made the force, but he had to straighten to get it off to Blake. As he did, the runner hit him, in that second lost by straightening. The collision jarred his throw and it went wild, into the Sox dugout. The tie-breaking run came in and the batter wound up on second.

The crowd hooted. The crowd jeered. All their derision was aimed at Bud, and up in the booth the official scorer charged him with an error on a wild throw.

He turned and just looked at Devlin. Devlin looked at him, frankly sneering, and said, "What's the matter? Tighten up, or what?"

Herb Ward, looking dejected, faced the next hitter, and Bud went back to position. Herb pitched angrily, and on the third one the batter popped a high, lazy fly to Valenti and that ended the inning.

The score was 4 to 3 now. Three outs to go.

This time, at last, the Sox simply didn't have another last-ditch stand left in them. That missed double play seemed to have crushed the something in them that had carried them along these past two weeks.

Bud flied out to center. Willie (the Lion) Simms, pinch-hitting for Herb Ward, lined to short. And Madigan grounded meekly to third. So that was the end of the ball game, the end of the winning streak, the end of the chance to take first place—and the end of Bud Walker.

The gloom in the dressing room was as heavy as cheap perfume. Bud undressed slowly and he waited for his shower until he saw Devlin go in. Then he followed him.

Devlin looked around when he walked in. They were alone. Bud said, "Why didn't you feed it to me right, Devlin?"

"Don't alibi yourself, busher," Devlin said. "You missed the D. P. You lost the game. So what? It's just another ball game. We've got plenty more to win."

"You had time, Devlin. You weren't rushed."

Devlin walked over. "Something tells me you want some trouble."

"Yeah," Bud said. "From you, I do. Finally."

Devlin swung and Bud brushed it off with his arm and swung back. He hit Devlin. Devlin swung and hit him. They both slipped on the wet floor and, panting, circled each other for the good opening.

From the doorway Jug Slavin said, "Now break it up."

Both dropped their arms. Both turned and stared and said nothing.

But Jug Slavin was feeling loquacious, for him. He said, "Well, this does it. I've warned you both. I've had enough of this stuff. Both of you get cleaned up, get out, and get back here early tomorrow—say, noon. I'll talk to O'Neill and we'll end this thing, once and for all, tomorrow. It's up to O'Neill, not me. One of you goes and one stays, and O'Neill will tell you which."

And that, Bud thought miserably, was a choice that was not too hard to guess. He saw Devlin's face break out into a happy grin as Slavin walked from the shower room.

CHAPTER

28

BUD MADE IT A POINT TO BE EARLY THE NEXT DAY, but Devlin was earlier. So was Jug Slavin and so was O'Neill. No one else was in evidence around the locker room, and Bud felt grateful for that. When you get the ax across the nape of the neck it is easier to take, somehow, without a sizable audience.

This was the final ax session, all right, the real thing. There was no doubt in his mind about that when he entered, and less than none after he had been there a few minutes. He knew where he stood with the front office just as well as he knew where he stood with the fans, who paid the money that supported the corporation that met the huge payroll of this star-studded team. He could have won if he had been fighting a human element; he was sure of that. But he couldn't lick a corporation.

There were no polite preliminaries, no build-up, no sparring for an opening. From the look on Dev-

lin's face Bud knew, even before O'Neill spoke,
that he was through as far as this team was concerned. It was a great team that he would hate to
leave, and they could beat anything, but he guessed
even a great team couldn't beat the front office.

"Walker," O'Neill said, "you're through on this
club."

"I know. I'll pack up."

"I'll tell you why."

"Don't bother. I know why."

O'Neill looked faintly baffled. He had probably
arisen early and rehearsed a dramatic speech, for
he was fond of making speeches. To be robbed of
the chance to make this one left him baffled and almost hurt, though a front-office heart is a difficult
thing to pierce.

Bud walked over to his locker and began to pull
his random possessions out, casually and without
dramatics.

That seemed to kindle a defensive spark in
O'Neill, who followed him in disconcerted wonder.
"Of course, Walker," he said, clearing his throat
gently, "we all admit you're a pretty good second
baseman."

"Thanks," Bud said.

"It's just that we happen to have a better one.
And you can't seem to get along in the same dugout
with Devlin, so. . . ."

Bud paused in his locker foray. He turned and looked at the Sox president. "Did you ever play ball, Mr. O'Neill?"

"Not professionally, no. I've been a businessman all my life, Walker. I built this club into a sound financial proposition and. . . ."

"I know all about that. I read it in the papers. And I wouldn't argue business with you, Mr. O'Neill, because I don't know very much about it. But I know a lot about a baseball team and what makes it tick. So when you tell me that Devlin is a better second baseman for this team than I am— well, I don't think it's true and I don't think the team thinks it's true."

O'Neill was so aghast that he was speechless.

"You pay their salaries, so they wouldn't argue with you about it. But it's a feeling with me. I know." Bud returned to the locker. "Not that it makes any difference," he added.

"You're a very smug young man, Walker. And a little mixed up about your value to this team."

"The next month's record of this team will show just how mixed up I am," Bud said. "Let's leave it that way." He kept on sorting things from the locker, never bothering to look at O'Neill when he spoke.

O'Neill's face kept getting redder and he started to say something as the door opened. Chip Fiske

walked in, followed by Eddie Lasky and Pete
Gibbs.

Chip took a look at the scene and said, "Hey,
Bud! What's up? What you doing?"

"I'm packing," Bud said.

"You leaving us?" Lasky asked.

Bud nodded.

Fiske, Lasky, and Gibbs walked over and stood
close to him. They looked at Slavin and then at
O'Neill. O'Neill cleared his throat again. He said,
"For the general good of this team, Walker is going
to one of our farm clubs. I'm sure you men understand why that is."

"No," Lasky said, "I don't understand it." He
looked at Fiske. Fiske looked at Gibbs.

Then Lasky, whose right arm had been the backbone of last year's pennant and would be the
backbone of this one's—if there were going to be one
—looked at O'Neill. And suddenly, from the way
Lasky was looking—and Fiske and Gibbs—Bud
knew that when you became part of a team, you
really did become a part of it. It was a feeling, and
it had nothing to do with official pronouncements.
It was a warm and human thing that even corpora-
tions couldn't beat down.

Lasky said, in a firm, clear voice, "I started out
this season as a pretty bad pitcher. This team
looked like a pretty bad team. We were missing

something to pull us together and we got it, when Walker started playing second base."

"Lasky. . . ." O'Neill began.

"Let me finish," Lasky said. "Every pitcher on this team found himself after Walker took over second base. The team found itself. The records show that. We won nine straight and jumped from fourth place to the top. The only reason the streak ended and we dropped from the top was because we missed a double play yesterday—at second base, when Walker wasn't playing second base."

"Listen," O'Neill said, "you're just a ballplayer, Lasky. If you want to shoot off your mouth. . . ."

Lasky walked away. He walked to his locker and fished the top part of his uniform out. He walked back to O'Neill and held it out.

"I'm not just a ballplayer talking," he said. "I think I'm the team talking. Walker is part of that team and we could win a pennant if you'd let us. But if you won't . . . well, here's my shirt. I'm not playing if Walker isn't."

O'Neill did not hold out his hands to receive it, so Lasky dropped it on the floor in front of him. The door opened again and Blake walked in, followed by Madigan, Bates, Valenti, and Ward.

"You can't break up a team," Lasky said, "to protect an investment. We may be pros, but we're still a team of human beings. We're not coupons. You can't clip us."

He stepped away and Fiske stepped up. Fiske had his shirt in hand, too. "And here's another uniform you can have," Fiske was saying.

Gibbs was right behind him. "And another," Gibbs said.

Madigan, Bates, Valenti, and Blake had formed a line. O'Neill stood there, looking helpless.

Jug Slavin said, "I'll have no team today, I guess."

O'Neill said incredulously, "Do all of you feel this strongly? You all think the team needs Walker this much?"

He got his answer from Lasky. "Yes," Lasky said. "Now you know what we're talking about. We're talking about a *team*."

It was a tie ball game going into the bottom half of the ninth. Bix Hanson had pitched shutout ball against the Grays, but they were still hungry for vindication and the Sox had not scored either.

Bates opened the ninth with a double. Gibbs grounded to second and Bates took third. Bud stepped in and the Grays' pitcher threw three straight balls, though not pitch-outs. Bud looked toward the third-base coaching box, expecting the take sign. But he didn't get it. He was free to hit, and in this spot he knew it meant that there was confidence in him, to the hilt. They believed he could bring that run in. He was their regular second baseman; he was no stand-in, no weak substitute that they had to put up with temporarily. All that humiliation, he knew from Tweet's sign, was behind him. For keeps.

The pitch came in and it wasn't the fourth ball. It was a strike. But he still didn't swing at it. He slid his hands down the handle of the bat and pushed the bat at it. No hero role for him; he wasn't a hero. He was just a team man, but he had found out a few short hours ago that, compared to a team man, a hero simply didn't rate.

It was a neat bunt. It dribbled down the first-base line, just inside. He legged it down the line, but he didn't really need to, because there would be no play on him. The play was on Bates, at the plate, and a futile play it was. Bates slid in with the run that meant the game, and they were off on what might prove to be another good long winning streak.

He heard a strange noise come from the stands as he trotted toward the players' gate. At first he couldn't identify it, it sounded so strange, so foreign. But then he remembered from way back, from Triple-A. It was a cheer. It was not a loud one, but it really was a cheer.

As he pushed through into the tunnel, he heard a fan in a seat behind the dugout yell, "We're off again! Nine straight again!"

They were finally beginning to accept him, and he guessed it was for the same reason that O'Neill

had accepted him. He was part of the team, and
the team could beat anybody: the Clippers, the
front office, even the fans who paid the freight.

In the locker room later, Jug Slavin walked over.
He looked relaxed for the first time all season. He
said, "Well, kid, now I've seen everything—fan
mutiny and team mutiny!"

"How did the Clippers do?" Bud asked.

"They lost."

"Then we're tied for first again."

"Yes. Listen, I just saw O'Neill for a minute.
Devlin's gone to a farm club. O'Neill is going to
peddle him for a fancy price so he'll save face with
his stockholders. That means the job is all yours
finally. Have a good year, kid."

"I will," Bud said. Words automatically formed
in his mouth, words he had sworn he would never
use again, because they always came back to mock
him. But this time, at last, he knew they wouldn't
mock him. So he used the same old refrain again.
But this time it wasn't whistling in the dark. This
time it was a statement of fact.

"It's my year, this year," he said.